PENGUIN CLASSICS

PIERRE AND JEAN

GUY DE MAUPASSANT was born in Normandy in 1850. At his parents' separation he stayed with his mother, who was a friend of Flaubert. As a young man he was lively and athletic, but the first symptoms of syphilis appeared in the late 1870s. By this time Maupassant had become Flaubert's pupil in the art of prose. On the publication of the first short story to which he put his name, *Boule de suif*, he left his job in the civil service and his temporary alliance with the disciples of Zola at Médan, and devoted his energy to professional writing. In the next eleven years he published dozens of articles, nearly three hundred stories and six novels, the best known of which are *A Woman's Life*, *Bel-Ami* and *Pierre and Jean*. He led a hectic social life, lived up to his reputation for womanizing and fought his disease. By 1889 his friends saw that his mind was in danger, and in 1891 he attempted suicide and was committed to an asylum in Paris, where he died two years later.

•

LEONARD TANCOCK spent most of his life in or near London, exceptions being a year as a student in Paris, most of the 1939–45 war in Wales, and three periods in American universities as visiting professor. He was a Fellow of University College London, and was formerly Reader in French at the university. From preparing his first Penguin Classic in 1949 he was intensely interested in problems of translation, about which he wrote, lectured and broadcast, and which he believed was an art rather than a science. His numerous translations for the Penguin Classics include Zola's *Germinal*, *Thérèse Raquin*, *The Debacle*, *L'Assommoir* and *La Bête Humaine*; Diderot's *The Nun*, *Rameau's Nephew* and *D'Alembert's Dream*; Marivaux's *Up from the Country*; Constant's *Adolphe*; La Rochefoucauld's *Maxims*; Voltaire's *Letters on England* and Madame de Sévigné's *Selected Letters*. Dr Tancock died in 1986 at the age of eighty-three.

GUY DE MAUPASSANT

PIERRE AND JEAN

TRANSLATED
WITH AN INTRODUCTION BY
LEONARD TANCOCK

PENGUIN BOOKS

PENGUIN BOOKS

Published by the Penguin Group
Penguin Books Ltd, 27 Wrights Lane, London W8 5TZ, England
Penguin Putnam Inc., 375 Hudson Street, New York, New York 10014, USA
Penguin Books Australia Ltd, Ringwood, Victoria, Australia
Penguin Books Canada Ltd, 10 Alcorn Avenue, Toronto, Ontario, Canada M4V 3B2
Penguin Books (NZ) Ltd, Private Bag 102902, NSMC, Auckland, New Zealand

Penguin Books Ltd, Registered Offices: Harmondsworth, Middlesex, England

This translation and introduction first published 1979
13

Introduction and translation copyright © Leonard Tancock, 1979
All rights reserved.

Printed in Great Britain by Antony Rowe Ltd, Chippenham, Wiltshire
Set in Monotype Bembo

CONTENTS

INTRODUCTION

GUY DE MAUPASSANT (1850–93), born in Normandy, near Dieppe, and all his life deeply attached to his native province and its coast, belonged to a family in comfortable circumstances, though his parents were on bad terms and after his early childhood he saw little of his father who, however, helped him after he grew up. His education was almost the standard one at such a social level – after local private schools and the Lycée Corneille at the provincial capital, Rouen, he began studying law in Paris at the age of nineteen. But this course was cut off by the outbreak of the war of 1870, when he went into the army. After his discharge and a certain amount of casting round and courting influential people, Maupassant got settled from 1872 in a modest Civil Service job in Paris, where he was to remain until literary success enabled him to stand on his own feet. But apart from some almost unnoticed poetry, or verse (the *sine qua non* for the young Frenchman at that time with literary ambitions), he published little until 1880. Then, with one short story, *Boule de suif*, he leaped from obscurity to the summit of art, where he remained as one of the undisputed masters of that most difficult genre, which indeed he still is.

The circumstances are well known but will bear repeating. Zola, now rich and famous, had bought a country house at Médan on the Seine, where he held court to a number of young admirers. His great ambition was to lead a movement and be the acknowledged master of what he called Naturalism. But he could never expect that men already eminent like Flaubert, Edmond de Goncourt or Daudet would meekly fall in behind his banner. So he conceived the generous and at the same time astute idea of publishing a collection of short stories, related because the subject of each was to be an incident of the 1870 war, each to be written by one of his young disciples, preceded by a story of his own and published at Zola's own personal risk by his publisher Charpentier. The authors were, in this order in the volume, Zola, Maupassant, Huysmans, Céard, Hennique and Zola's friend and first biographer, Alexis.

The volume appeared in 1880, in the same year as Zola's literary manifesto *Le Roman expérimental*, and was intended as an illustration and vindication of the theories in that book and other critical writings of Zola. But, remarkable though it was, Zola's own contribution, *L'Attaque du moulin*, was not the sensation. That was Maupassant's *Boule de suif*. Both are very great stories, but they are strongly contrasted, and in this contrast can be seen the originality of Maupassant's genius.

Both stories are based on real life. But for *L'Attaque du moulin* Zola used his usual method of accumulating authentic facts carefully stored in his notebooks, and then putting them together into a skilful, lifelike mosaic. Each element is a miracle of observation and realism, but the final effect is somewhat crowded with significant happenings, like a painting by Frith. On the other hand, for *Boule de suif* Maupassant took a real adventure witnessed by some people he knew, simplified it to the bare essentials of changeless human nature and placed it in a setting he knew perfectly, in this case the road from Rouen to Dieppe via Tôtes. And it reads naturally, like a simple tale told casually by one man to another. Neither has it any dramatic ending, for real life has no exit lines or final curtains; it just has to go on.

Yet the overnight success of *Boule de suif* is by no means as miraculous as it might seem. It is the fruit of a long apprenticeship which surely must be unique in literature. As he generously points out in the preface to *Pierre et Jean* entitled *Le Roman*, he became from his early twenties the friend whom the lonely and ageing Flaubert loved as a son. Flaubert was never too tired or busy to look through Maupassant's work and discuss it with him at length, and he even set him literary tasks to do and went

8

through them with him like a tutor with a student's essay. Moreover Flaubert continually warned him not to publish too soon. Maupassant's art is therefore the product of many years of training by one of the greatest stylists and most fastidious artists in French literature.

From the moment of publishing *Boule de suif* Maupassant produced an enormous amount of journalism, short stories and six novels, mostly in ten years, for by 1890 there were unmistakable signs of mental deterioration, syphilitic in origin, and he died in an institution in 1893, of general paralysis of the insane. He was the least professional of writers, for all the time he led an active and feverish life as a fashionable man about town (like Bel-Ami), interspersed with luxurious holidays, yachts on the Mediterranean and all kinds of extravagance. He even affected not to do any writing unless he had run out of money, which of course, given his way of life, was a chronic condition.

In the seven or eight years between 1883 and 1890 Maupassant produced six novels of uneven quality, of which *Pierre et Jean* (1888) was the fourth. If such a thing as a scale of values had any meaning one could say that it is the greatest. It is certainly a flawless work of art, for in it he avoids the two pitfalls facing a master of the short story when he tries to write a novel. On the one hand, accustomed as he is to practising economy, compression, suppression of all irrelevant matter, the short-story writer tends to string together a number of episodes or short stories round a central character and call the result a novel, or on the other to take a simple story and pad it out with descriptive matter and side-issues. On the whole Maupassant had learned his lessons from Flaubert too well to indulge in mere padding and inflation, but his first novel, *Une Vie* (1883), can fairly be called an album of sketches or incidents, things that happen to the heroine, Jeanne.

Bel-Ami (1885), although in a sense written to a similar formula – episodes, some of them re-workings of stories of his own, grouped round a central character – is far more successful as a novel. For one thing, the central figure, Georges Duroy, is male and in some ways extremely like Guy de Maupassant, and he is very much alive. For another, this is the old and well-tried theme of the young man who by his wits, good looks and sexual attraction makes his way in the world with the help of wealthy or influential women, like Jacob in Marivaux's *Le Paysan parvenu*, Stendhal's Julien Sorel, Balzac's Rastignac and very recently Zola's Octave Mouret. But above all, the method of accumulation of episodes is peculiarly suitable for a social study of the shady world of venal journalism, tricky finance and politics, the world of such Trollopian characters as Melmotte or Quintus Slide. In this sense *Bel-Ami* is a realist or naturalist novel of observation of a particular social type, trade or profession, like the Rougon-Macquart novels of Zola.

Mont-Oriol (1887) is the weakest of Maupassant's novels, but it is of interest that he put into it two things which he will treat to perfection a year later in *Pierre et Jean*: the theme of doubtful paternity, almost an obsession with Maupassant, and the use of description, in this case of the Auvergne, as an expression of mood or atmosphere. The last two novels, *Fort comme la mort* and *Notre cœur* (1889 and 1890), need not concern us here. They are to some extent novels of high society or the *demi-monde*, they are, in spite of what Maupassant says in *Le Roman*, psychological novels, but they work because the hero is in each case clearly Guy de Maupassant himself and he projected into them some of the tragedy of his own premonitions of on-coming collapse and artistic sterility.

Some time has been spent on the novels preceding *Pierre et Jean*, and notably on *Bel-Ami*, because Maupassant prefaced *Pierre et Jean* with an important article entitled *Le Roman*, a stocktaking of his own position and a literary manifesto. He goes out of his way in the opening lines to make it clear that the novel which follows, i.e. *Pierre et Jean*, is not a good example of what he is about to propose, in fact that if anything it might work against his theories. His subject is rather generalities about the novel, an attack upon hidebound critics, a very broad statement of what the novel should be and a declaration of personal faith in art. It is because this preface applies so obviously to the art of *Bel-Ami* and not to that of *Pierre et Jean* that Douglas Parmée rightly analyses it at some length in the introduction to his translation of *Bel-Ami* (Penguin Classics, 1974). The reader is referred to pp. 9–12 of that introduction. But as a translation of the article appears in its rightful place as the preface to this volume it cannot be ignored here.

The style, with its curiously amateurish or schoolboyish over-emphasis, repetitions, lists of near-synonyms and similar devices, is strangely different from the sober economy of the novel it purports to introduce. I have attempted to show this in my translation. Maupassant begins with a salvo against blinkered academic critics who insist upon judging and classifying an artist's work, not by what he is trying to do, but according to some notion of 'the rules' or 'the genre' (an endemic condition in French criticism throughout the ages), but who in reality are merely dressing up their personal likes and dislikes in impressive jargon. This leads to his insisting upon the absolute freedom of the artist to choose his own subject and his manner of treating it. Maupassant always remained fiercely independent in the sense that he refused to join any group, whether political, religious or artistic, that would tie him down. So although, as he points out in this preface, he has no use for emotionalism and romantic feeling, because it distorts truth and portrays abnormal types, but demands facts and ordinary, average humanity, yet he refuses to be classified with the Naturalists and their untenable scientific claims. For Realism allied to pseudo-science leads to catalogues of boring facts and objects, without selection, and that is the very opposite of art. There must be choice, and that choice must be personal. There is no ultimate reality, only the particular novelist's reality as he sees it through his own eyes, for they are all he has. Therefore the novel of psychological analysis is nonsense, for we cannot read any other human being's mind; all we do is project our own minds into the characters. The characters in a psychological novel are of necessity the author wearing different hats. The only recourse open to the novelist is external observation to suggest internal action. The novelist is not omniscient, and must present in his characters what other men could see, and no more.

This last point leads Maupassant naturally to Flaubert who, he says, taught him all this and above all the importance of simplicity and aptness in writing. And before closing he attacks, not by name, but nothing could be more obvious, the elaborate, ornate, fussy style made fashionable by the Goncourt brothers and still championed by Edmond, the surviving brother, the style full of abstract nouns and exotic, highly technical and incomprehensible words, known as l'écriture artiste.

Such a sweeping condemnation of the so-called psychological novel and demand for nothing but visible facts and appearances would seem to be the very opposite of what he does in Pierre et Jean. He had admitted this in Le Roman, and indeed it is part and parcel of the absolute freedom he demands for the artist. Whereas Bel-Ami concerns itself with a large section of society, Pierre et Jean is an intensely personal novel that plays itself out in a small, closed circle, a family of four with four or five subsidiary characters, one of whom is destined to become 'family' by marriage. The action is mostly in the mind of Pierre, the elder son, and towards the end in that of Jean, his brother. Nor in any strict sense can it be said that Maupassant uses observation of external things to suggest inner mental processes, for most of the agonized thinking of Pierre is at lonely times of inaction: when he is lying in bed, gazing out at the dark sea from the harbour arm, sitting on a bench apparently day dreaming, lying on the shingle. And the crucial bit of heart-searching on the part of Jean is done when he is lying fully dressed on a settee in his new home, from the small hours until the morning is far advanced; then he goes out and acts upon the decision he has reached. That act is a result of his long cogitation, but it cannot be said to be an external sign of his thought-processes. None of this psychological action would be noticeable to an outside observer, however acute. He would simply see a man doing nothing.

Yet there is a link between Maupassant's theory of observable facts and the development in Pierre's mind of suspicion and then certainty. He cannot understand himself, but is always fumbling forward under the influence of events outside himself – atmospheres, sounds, sights, lights in the darkness, fogs and mists, symbols of all kinds.

It is the skill and economy of means with which Maupassant shows these events and experiences working on Pierre's state of mind that make this short novel a masterpiece of construction. In a classical play the data are set out at once: a small group of people in a closed environment. Their characters are different and their aims may be opposed, the situation may have explosive possibilities but for the moment it is stable. There comes some outside event affecting their fortunes, often a piece of news, true or false, and at once the ingredients become active and the characters begin to work on each other until an intolerable situation leads to catastrophe. This is exactly the position in *Pierre et Jean*. In a small boat off Le Havre is a family of four. Roland, the father, is just a silly old man (the very first word in the book, a schoolgirl expletive, betrays him), obtuse, amiable unless crossed, when he is given to petulant explosions that nobody takes any notice of. Mme Roland, the mother, still attractive, rather sentimental and given to reading novels and poetry, seems more intelligent than her husband, whose irritable little outbursts she tactfully deals with. The grown-up sons, home for the holidays, are sharply contrasted, not only in character, the one nervy and excitable, the other equable and morally lazy, but physically, the elder sinewy and dark, the younger bigger, softer-looking and fair. Between the two there is clearly the sort of rivalry and almost unrecognized jealousy that exists in most families. But here in the boat they are being watched by a fifth person, a young and attractive widow with whom both brothers are on flirting terms, and at this moment scoring off each other by trying to impress her with their prowess at rowing or fishing. At once on their return home there comes from their family lawyer the piece of news which sets the drama in motion. An old family friend, M. Maréchal, whom nobody has seen or heard of for some years, has died and left his entire fortune to the younger son, Jean. Why? Of the four, one doesn't bother to think, one knows, one has strong suspicions and the last, the legatee, is stunned and postpones thinking.

From the moment of the arrival of the news in the Roland household the machine begins to move and each actor's tendencies and relationships to the others, already visible, but only just, become intensified and active. The father's shallow *bonhomie* turns into garrulous glee and plans for celebrations, the mother, apprehensive, shrinks into a protective shell of dreams, Pierre becomes sarcastic and plainly jealous, Jean is inclined to wait and see. From now on every chance remark, every happening, however trivial, adds its weight to the growing certainty in Pierre's mind that Jean is Maréchal's child, and at the same time adds to the wretched mother's certainty that her elder son has guessed the truth. In his distress Pierre becomes increasingly cruel to his mother, whose fear of him turns her into a nervous wreck. Jean, meanwhile, prospers in his own affairs, and seemingly without effort gets the things Pierre would have liked. He is setting himself up in his luxurious new flat and spending less and less time at home. Father's only reaction to the disintegration of the family is odd explosions of irritability at such disasters as the lateness of the dinner. The old man's every word is a masterpiece of irony, for he alone is unaware of the sinister double meaning of so many of his remarks. In fact he knows nothing of what is going on and remains amiably stupid to the very end. Irony, bitter or comic, is exceedingly difficult to do unobtrusively, and to call attention to it in any way is as bad as explaining a joke. Often in novels and plays the ironies are so obvious that they might as well be labelled. In this novel, never. The remarks, especially of old Roland, are perfectly in character, and the harmless meaning, the face-value one, springs naturally from the events or circumstances of the story.

It is not without interest, given the immense influence of Flaubert upon Guy de Maupassant, that two of the former's later novels could similarly be sub-titled 'the story of a legacy'. In *L'Education sentimentale* a very ordinary provincial young man is enabled by a legacy to leave home in search of life, love and adventure in Paris. Conversely and ironically, in *Bouvard et Pécuchet* two humdrum, middle-aged Paris office workers, thanks to a legacy received by one of them, can leave their drab life on office stools and go to the country in search of leisure, nature, 'culture' and various other will-o'-the-wisps.

Yet this is not a plain tale of jealousy. Were it so Pierre's trouble would not be so acute, nor would the reader have any interest in him, for instead of anguish there would have been mere nastiness. This anguish comes from the deep love he has for his mother, and respect amounting to worship, for both boys owe her everything, given the weakness and nullity of the father. We hurt those we love, and he is impelled in spite of himself to hurt the person he loves most in the world, and her cringing pain lashes him into further cruelties. Also, in his own way, he loves his brother Jean. So he despises himself for his suspicions and jealousies, fights against them even while finding fresh food for them, and is horrified and overcome with remorse when in a moment of anger with his brother he blurts them out. But there is no melodrama. Some artists, Zola for instance, might at this point have brought in violence or even death by way of a dénouement. Not so Maupassant, who knows that in real life nothing lasts, a new *modus vivendi* has to be found, things have to go on. Events having come to an impossible pass, Pierre lets himself be guided into a job which takes him away, and his ship fades out in the haze of an autumn day. Throughout the story the atmospheres, sounds and sights of a busy seaport and the neighbouring coast and hinterland sometimes comment on the action and sometimes intervene to turn the action in a new direction. Sea mists and fogs, shipping entering and leaving the port or anchored while waiting for the tide, lighthouses, lights moving in the darkness, shrieking sirens and moaning foghorns, all play their parts and prompt certain thoughts and emotions in people's minds. When, for example, Pierre escapes from his mental torments by taking the boat out on a lovely summer day with only Papagris, the hired sailor, he has a sensation of peace, sanity and happiness, but this is suddenly shattered by a fog that rushes down from nowhere and chases him back into his life of hell. This world of symbols is of course the personal touch of Maupassant, a born Norman soaked in the atmosphere of this part of Normandy round the Seine estuary between Caen and Fécamp, who wrote the novel at his house at Étretat. Seldom are we unaware of the smell of brine, tar and fish or the screaming of gulls, unless it be in a trip inland among the cornfields and orchards of the rich country-side. And one of the major scenes takes place at the foot of chalk cliffs amid the scrub and boulders from ancient landslides in a place exactly like the Warren, between Dover and Folkestone.

What has been said so far might suggest that *Pierre et Jean* is a depressing tale of unrelieved gloom, nervous tension and family disintegration. It is not. Here once again Maupassant shows his belief that in real life nothing is undiluted and permanent. Sooner or later the trivial and ridiculous, the boring or embarrassing break in. For so short a novel on so grim a subject there is an astonishing amount of humour in dialogue, in description, in situation. The miracle is that in so small a compass so many possibilities are touched on without distracting attention from the main theme. Nothing is unduly stressed but so much is suggested. Like a great poem it can be re-read many times before its implications are exhausted or its strange power loses its hold.

NOTE ON THIS TRANSLATION

I have used as a working text that of the Classiques Garnier edition, edited by Pierre Cogny, and collated this with the Conard edition of the *Œuvres complètes de Guy de Maupassant*. Both editions reproduce the text of the first edition, published by Paul Ollendorff, 1888.

September 1976   L.W.T.

The Novel

The Novel

I DO not intend to make any plea here for the little novel which follows. Quite the opposite; the ideas I am going to try to make clear would if anything lead to hostile criticism of the kind of psychological study I have undertaken in *Pierre and Jean*.

I want to deal with the Novel in general.

I am not the only person at whom the same accusation is directed by the same critics every time a new book appears.

In the midst of flattering phrases I regularly find this one from the same pens:

'The great flaw in this work is that it is not a novel in the proper sense of the word.'

One could answer back with the same argument:

'The great flaw in the writer who does me the honour of judging me is that he is not a critic.'

What, then, are the necessary qualities of a critic?

Without bias, preconceived notions, ideas from any 'school', ties with any family of artists, he must understand, distinguish and explain all the most contrasting tendencies, the most dissimilar temperaments and accept the most diverse artistic aims.

Now the critic who, after *Manon Lescaut*, *Paul et Virginie*, *Don Quixote*, *Les Liaisons dangereuses*, *Werther*, *Elective Affinities*, *Clarissa Harlowe*, *Emile*, *Candide*, *Cinq-Mars*, *René*, *The Three Musketeers*, *Mauprat*, *Le Père Goriot*, *La Cousine Bette*, *Colomba*, *Le Rouge et le Noir*, *Mademoiselle de Maupin*, *Notre-Dame de Paris*, *Salammbô*, *Madame Bovary*, *Adolphe*, *M. de Camors*, *L'Assommoir*, *Sapho*, etc., still dares to write: 'This is a novel, that is not', seems to me to be endowed with a perspicacity suspiciously like incompetence.

Usually this critic understands by the term 'novel' a more or less credible adventure arranged rather like a play in three acts, the first of which contains the exposition, the second the action and the third the dénouement.

This method of construction is perfectly valid on condition that all the others are equally accepted.

Are there any rules for writing a novel which must be observed, or else a story should bear another name?

If *Don Quixote* is a novel, is *Le Rouge et le Noir* one as well? If *Monte-Cristo* is a novel, is *L'Assommoir* one? Can we establish any comparison between Goethe's *Elective Affinities*, Dumas's *The Three Musketeers*, Flaubert's *Madame Bovary*, M. O. Feuillet's *M. de Camors* and M. Zola's *Germinal?* Which of these works is a novel? What are these famous rules? Where do they come from? Who drew them up? By virtue of what principle, what authority, what reasoning?

Yet it seems that these critics know for certain, without any doubt whatsoever, what constitutes a novel and what differentiates it from something else that isn't one. Put plainly, this means that without being productive themselves they have formed a school and, like the novelists, reject any books conceived and executed outside their own aesthetic system.

An intelligent critic should, on the contrary, look out for whatever is least like novels already written, and as much as possible encourage young people to try out new ways.

All writers, Victor Hugo as much as M. Zola, have persistently demanded the absolute, indisputable right to compose – that is to imagine or observe – in accordance with their personal conception of art. Talent comes from originality, which is a special way of thinking, seeing, understanding and judging. Now the critic who claims to define the Novel according to the notion he has formed of it from the novel he likes, and to establish certain unchangeable rules of composition, will every time come up against an artistic temperament introducing some new technique. A critic really worthy of the name should be simply an analyst, without bias, without preferences, without passions and, like an expert in pictures, should only appraise the artistic value of the work of art submitted to him. His under-standing, open to everything, should so override his own personality that he can reveal and praise even books that as a man he dislikes and that as a judge he is obliged to comprehend.

But the majority of critics are merely readers, and hence it comes about that they find fault with us almost always for the wrong reason or pat us on the back without reservation or moderation.

The reader of a book who is looking only for the satisfaction of his own turn of mind asks the writer to cater for his predom-inant taste, and always calls a work or a passage remarkable or well written when it appeals to his own imagination, whether that be idealistic, gay, prurient, sad, dreamy or positive.

In fact, the public is made up of many groups who cry out:

'Console me.'

'Amuse me.'

'Make me sad.'

'Make me feel sentimental.'

'Make me dream.'

'Make me shudder.'

'Make me weep.'

'Make me think.'

Only a few choice spirits ask the artist:

'Do something beautiful in the form that suits you best according to your own temperament.'

The artist tries, succeeds or fails.

The critic should judge the result only in relation to the nature of the effort; he has no right to concern himself with trends.

This has been written a thousand times already. It always has to be repeated.

So, after literary schools that have been determined to give us a deformed, superhuman, poetic, sentimental, charming or sublime vision of life, there has developed a realist and natur-alist school that has claimed to show us truth, nothing but the truth, the whole truth.

One must accept with equal interest these vastly different theories of art and judge the works they produce solely from the point of view of their artistic worth, accepting *a priori* the general ideas that gave them birth.

To contest an author's right to create a poetic or realistic work is to want to force him to change his temperament, challenge his originality, refuse to allow him to use the eye and the intelligence nature has given him.

To blame him for seeing things as beautiful or ugly, small or epic, appealing or sinister, is to blame him for being warped in some way and not seeing things in the same way as we do.

Let him stay free to understand, observe and conceive as he thinks fit, provided he be an artist. If we are judging an idealist let us rise to poetic heights and then demonstrate to him that his dream is ordinary, commonplace, not sufficiently frenzied or magnificent. But if we are judging a naturalist let us show him in what way the truth in real life differs from the truth in his book.

It is obvious that such contrasted schools have had to employ completely opposite methods of composition.

The novelist who transforms the unchanging, brutish, unpleasant truth in order to extract from it an exceptional and charming story must, without worrying too much about plausibility, manipulate events for his own purposes, prepare and arrange them in order to please, thrill or touch the heart of the reader. The plan of his novel is simply a series of ingenious devices leading skilfully to the dénouement. The incidents are set out and graduated to lead to the culminating point and effect of the conclusion which is a crowning and decisive event, satisfying all the curiosities awakened at the outset, closing the interest and so completely terminating the story that the reader no longer wants to know what will happen tomorrow to even the most attractive characters.

But on the other hand the novelist who claims to give us an accurate picture of life must carefully avoid any linking of events likely to seem exceptional. His aim is not to tell us a story, amuse or touch our hearts, but to force us to think and understand the profound, hidden meaning of the events. Through having observed and meditated he looks at the universe, things, facts and mankind in a certain way which is his own and the result of his own observations and deliberation. It is this personal view of the world that he is trying to communicate to us by reproducing it in a book. In order to touch our emotions as he himself has been touched by the spectacle of life, he must reproduce it before our eyes with scrupulous accuracy. So he must put his work together in such a skilful, hidden and apparently artless way that it is impossible to perceive and state what the plan is and discover his intentions.

Instead of contriving an adventure and unfolding it so as to make it absorbing right to the end, he will take his character or characters at a certain stage in their existence and lead them to the next stage by natural transitions. In this way he will demonstrate sometimes how people are modified through the influence of the circumstances in which they find themselves, sometimes how feelings and passions develop, how people love or hate, how they struggle in all the social environments, how bourgeois, financial, family or political interests clash.

The skill of his plan will not therefore consist in emotion or charm, in a beguiling opening or thrilling catastrophe, but in the ingenious grouping of changeless little facts from which the real meaning of the work will emerge. If he is to get into three hundred pages ten years of a life in order to show what its salient and characteristic significance has been in the midst of all the human beings with whom that life has been surrounded, he must know how to eliminate from the innumerable small daily events all those that do not serve his purpose, and throw into relief in a special way all those that might have remained unnoticed by unobservant onlookers, and which give the book its meaning and value as a whole.

It can be seen that such a method of composition, very different from the old method visible to all, often throws critics off the track, for they do not detect all the fine, hidden and almost invisible threads used by certain modern artists instead of the single piece of string that used to be called 'the plot'.

In a word, if the Novelist of yesterday selected and narrated the crises of life, the abnormal states of the soul and heart, the Novelist of today writes the history of the heart, soul and mind in their normal state. In order to produce the effect he is aiming at, namely the feeling of simple reality, and to extract from it the artistic lesson he wants, that is the revelation of what the contemporary man before his very eyes really is, he must limit himself to facts irrefutably and invariably true.

But even if we look at things from the point of view of these realist artists themselves, one must discuss and contest their theory, which looks as though it could be summed up in these words: nothing but the truth and the whole truth.

Their object being to discover the philosophy underlying certain constant and common facts, they will often have to modify events for the sake of plausibility and to the detriment of truth, for

Le vrai peut quelquefois n'être pas vraisemblable.*

The realist, if he is an artist, will try not to show us a commonplace photograph of life, but to give us a more complete view of it, more striking, more convincing than reality itself.

To tell all would be impossible, for it would necessitate at least a volume per day to enumerate the multitudes of insignificant incidents that fill our lives.

So a choice has to be made, and this is the first blow to the theory of the whole truth.

Moreover life is made up of the most differing, unforeseen,

*Literally 'the true can sometimes lack verisimilitude'. From Boileau: *L'Art poétique* (1669–74), the great apologia for French classicism. The line is an implied criticism of the Corneille practice of 'guaranteeing' the accuracy of improbable occurrences by quoting historical sources. With typical common sense Maupassant insists that all art consists of selection and rejection from the raw material of life. He is attacking some of the self-styled scientific realists of the Zola school, though not Zola himself.

contradictory, ill-assorted things; it is brutal, arbitrary, disconnected, full of inexplicable, illogical and contradictory disasters which can only be classified under the heading of 'Other news in brief.'

That is why the artist, having chosen his theme, will select from this life, cluttered as it is with hazards and silly little things, only the characteristic details useful for his subject, and he will reject all the rest, all the side-issues.

One example out of a thousand:

The number of people in the world who die in accidents every day is considerable. But can we drop a tile on the head of a principal character or throw him under the wheels of a bus in the middle of a story on the pretext that one must allow for accidents?

Life, moreover, puts everything on the same level, hurries events on or drags them out indefinitely. Art, on the contrary, consists in looking ahead and making preparations, managing skilful, disguised transitions, throwing full light, by literary skill alone, on the essential events while giving to all the others the amount of relief they deserve in accordance with their importance, so as to produce the profound sense of special truth it is desired to reveal.

Revealing the truth consists, therefore, in giving a total illusion of truth following the normal logic of events, not in transcribing them slavishly in the order in which they happen to occur.

I conclude from all this that the Realists of genius should really be called Illusionists.

In any case how childish it is to believe in reality when each one of us has his own reality in his thoughts and bodily organs. The eyes, ears, sense of smell and taste of each of us create as many truths as there are men on earth. And our minds, receiving instructions from these organs which are themselves influenced in different ways, understand, analyse and judge as though each one of us belonged to a different race.

So each of us simply creates for himself an illusion of the

world which may be poetic, sentimental, joyful or melancholy, sordid or lugubrious according to his nature. And the writer has no other mission than to reproduce this illusion faithfully with all the artistic techniques he has learned and can bring to bear.

Illusion of the beautiful – a human convention! Illusion of the ugly – changing opinion! Illusion of truth – never stable! Illusion of the vile which attracts so many people! The great artists are those who impose their personal illusion upon humanity.

So it behoves us not to take exception to any theory since each one is simply a generalized expression of a temperament analysing itself.

There are two theories in particular that have often been discussed by opposing them to each other instead of admitting both: that of the novel of psychological analysis pure and simple and that of the objective novel. The partisans of analysis expect the writer to concentrate upon plotting out the tiniest developments of a mind and all the most secret motives which determine one's actions, giving only minor importance to an actual happening. A happening is the destination, a simple milestone, the pretext for the novel. According to this school of thought such works, at one and the same time precise and visionary, in which imagination is wedded to observation, should be written in the same way as a philosopher composes a treatise on psychology, by setting out causes and tracing them back to their remotest origins, explaining all the reasons and desires and discerning every reaction of a soul motivated by self-interest, passion or instinct.

On the other hand the partisans of objectivity (hideous word!) aim at giving us an exact representation of what takes place in life, carefully avoiding any complicated explanation, any dissertation upon motives, and they limit themselves to showing us people and the things that happen.

In their view, the psychology should be concealed in the book as it is in reality behind the events of life.

The novel conceived in this manner gains intensity, speed of narrative, colour and the bustle of life.

Therefore instead of explaining at great length the state of mind of a character, objective writers seek out the action or gesture which such a state of mind must inevitably make this man perform in a given situation. And they make him behave in such a way throughout the book that all his acts and movements are reflections of his inner nature, of all his thoughts, all his desires or hesitations. Thus they hide psychology instead of displaying it, they make it the framework of the novel just as the invisible skeleton is the framework of the human body. The painter who paints our portrait does not display our skeleton.

Moreover I feel that a novel executed in this way gains in sincerity. To begin with it is more credible, for people we see in action round us don't tell us the motives that govern them.

Next we must bear in mind that even if through observing men we can determine their nature accurately enough to foresee how they will behave in almost any circumstances, even if we can say with certainty: 'Such a man, with such a temperament, in such a case, will do this,' it does not follow at all that we can determine, one by one, all the hidden stages in his thought, which is not our thought, all the mysterious urgings of his instincts, which are not the same as ours, all the complex promptings of his nature, the organs, nerves, blood and flesh of which are different from ours.

Whatever the genius of a man, meek, gentle, without passions, who loves only knowledge and work, he will never be able to transport himself completely enough into the soul and body of some exuberant, sensual, violent fellow who is excited by every desire and even by every vice, and understand and point out the most intimate compulsions and sensations of such a different being, even though he can perfectly well foresee and narrate all the actions of his life.

In fact, the man who goes in for pure psychology can only substitute himself for all his characters in the various situations

29

into which he puts them, for it is impossible for him to change his own organs, which are the only intermediaries between the outer world and ourselves, which impose their impressions upon us, determine our sensibility and create in us a soul essentially different from all those that surround us. We cannot help transferring some part of our own vision and knowledge of the world, acquired through the help of our senses and ideas about life, to all the characters whose innermost and unknown being we claim to lay bare. So it is always ourselves we show in the body of a king, a murderer, a thief or an honest man, a whore or a nun, a young girl or a fishwife in the market, for we are obliged to put the problem to ourselves in this way: 'If *I* were a king, a murderer, a thief, a whore, a nun, girl or fishwife, what would *I* do, what would *I* think, how would *I* act?' And so the only way we diversify our characters is by changing the age, sex, social position and all the circumstances of life of *our own personality* which nature has surrounded with an impenetrable barrier of natural organs.

The skill consists in not letting the reader recognize this *personality* behind all the masks we use to hide it.

But if pure psychological analysis is questionable from the point of view of complete accuracy, it can none the less give us works of art as perfect as any other method of work.

Today, for instance, we have the Symbolists. Why not? Their vision as artists is worthy of respect and they have the specially interesting quality that they do proclaim the extreme difficulty of art.

Indeed a man must be very crazy, very daring, very conceited or very silly to be writing at all today! After so many writers with such varied natures, such multifarious genius, what remains to be done that hasn't already been done or to be said that hasn't already been said? Which of us can flatter himself that he has written a page, or even a sentence, that cannot be found in almost the same form somewhere else? When people like ourselves read something, so saturated as we are with French writing that our whole body feels like a paste made of words, do we ever find a line or thought that is unfamiliar, which we have not thought of at least in a confused sort of way?

The man only concerned with keeping his public amused by time-honoured means, writes with confidence, in the innocence of his mediocrity, works intended for ignorant people wanting something to distract them. But those who feel weighed down by all the centuries of past literature, whom nothing will satisfy, to whom everything is distasteful because their own dreams are better, for whom everything seems deflowered and who feel that their work always looks like useless and common-place toil, come to consider the art of literature an intangible and mysterious thing of which only a few pages of the greatest masters give us a fleeting glimpse.

A score of lines of poetry or sentences suddenly discovered pierce us to the heart like an amazing revelation, but the lines that follow are like any other lines, and the prose that flows on afterwards like any bits of prose.

Men of genius may never go through these agonies and torments because they have within them an irresistible creative drive. They do not sit in judgement upon themselves. The others, the rest of us, who are simply conscientious and tireless workers, can only struggle against this invincible discourage-ment by unrelenting effort.

Two men, by their simple, illuminating teaching, have given me this strength to go on trying: Louis Bouilhet and Gustave Flaubert.

If I now speak of them and myself, it is because their advice, condensed into a few lines, will perhaps be of use to some young men with less confidence in themselves than one usually has when starting to write.

Bouilhet, whom I knew first in an intimate way about two years before gaining the friendship of Flaubert, by reiterating that a hundred lines or even fewer suffice for the reputation of an artist provided they are faultless and contain the essence of the talent and originality even of a second-rate man, made me understand that continual work and thorough technical

31

knowledge can, on a day of lucidity, power and inspiration, and happily married to a subject perfectly in keeping with all the tendencies of the writer's mind, bring about the burgeoning of a short, unique work as perfect as we can produce.

Next I understood that the most celebrated writers have hardly ever left more than a single volume, and that above all we must have the good fortune to find and recognize amid the multitude of subjects offering themselves to our choice, the one which will utilize all our abilities, all that is of value in us and all our artistic power.

Later on Flaubert, whom I saw occasionally, took a liking to me. I ventured to submit a few of my attempts. He read them kindly and said: 'I don't know whether you will have any talent. What you have brought to me proves you have some intelligence, but don't forget this, young man, that talent, as Chateaubriand* said, is simply long patience. Work.'

I did work, and often returned to him, realizing that he approved of me, for he had begun to call me jokingly his disciple.

For seven years I did poetry, I did tales or short stories, and even an appalling drama. None of this has survived. The master read it all, and then the following Sunday over a meal he developed his criticisms and little by little he drove into me two or three principles which are the essence of his long and patient instructions: 'If you have originality,' he would say, 'you must above all set it free, if not, you must acquire it.'

Talent is long patience. It is a matter of looking at anything you want to express long enough and closely enough to discover in it some aspect that nobody has yet seen or described. In everything there is an unexplored element because we are prone by habit to use our eyes only in combination with the memory of what others before us have thought about the

*This should read Buffon. The original edition gives Chateaubriand, which Garnier reproduces, but with a note that Maupassant himself realized at once that he had made a silly mistake. The Conard edition gives Buffon, with no explanation.

thing we are looking at. The most insignificant thing contains some little unknown element. We must find it. To describe a fire burning or a tree on a plain let us stand in front of that fire and that tree until for us they no longer look like any other tree or any other fire.

It is in this way that we become original.

Moreover, having propounded this truth that there do not exist in the whole world two grains of sand, two flies, two hands or two noses exactly similar, he forced me to express in a few sentences a being or an object so as to define it clearly and distinguish it from every other being or object of the same race or kind.

'When,' he said, 'you go past a grocer sitting at his door or a concierge smoking his pipe, or a cab rank, show me that grocer and that concierge, the position they take up, their whole physical appearance, containing, moreover, thanks to the skill of the picture, their whole moral nature so that I cannot confuse them with any other grocer or any other concierge, and make me see in a single word how one cab-horse is distinct from the fifty others in front of it and behind.'

I have set out elsewhere his ideas on style. They are closely related to the theory of observation I have just expounded.

Whatever we want to convey, there is only one word to express it, one verb to animate it, one adjective to qualify it. We must therefore go on seeking that word, verb or adjective until we have discovered it, and never be satisfied with approximations, never fall back on tricks, even inspired ones, or tomfoolery of language to dodge the difficulty.

The subtlest things can be expressed and described by applying this line of Boileau:

D'un mot mis en sa place enseigna le pouvoir.

There is no need for the outlandish, complicated, elaborate and Chinese vocabulary being forced upon us today, and called *l'écriture artiste*, in order to seize all the fine distinctions of thought. But one must distinguish with the utmost clearness all the modifications in the value of a word according to the position it occupies. Let us have fewer nouns, verbs and adjectives with almost indefinable meanings, but more phrases that are differentiated, varied in construction, ingeniously cut up, full of sonorities and subtle rhythms. Let us strive to be excellent stylists rather than collectors of rare words.*

It is in fact more difficult to handle a sentence as one wants, make it say everything, even what it does not express, fill it with suggestions, secret, unformulated intentions, than to invent novel expressions or dig out of old, unknown books all the ones that are no longer used, have lost their meaning and become for us so much dead verbiage.

It must be said also that the French language is like pure water that the mannered writers have never succeeded in muddying and never will. Each century has thrown into this limpid stream its fashions, its pretentious archaisms and its affectations, but none of these useless attempts and puny efforts have survived. The nature of this language is to be clear, logical and sinewy. It will not let itself be weakened, obscured or corrupted.

Those who nowadays go in for imagery without being careful about abstract terms, who make hail or rain fall upon the *cleanliness* of window-panes, are nice ones to throw stones

---

*This paragraph, and indeed all the rest of this preface, is an attack upon Edmond de Goncourt (1822-96) and upon the theory and practice of this writer and his brother Jules (1830-70). Until the latter's early death these two worked in one of the closest collaborations in literary history. They wrote important studies in eighteenth century art and 'discovered' the Far East, notably Japan. The 'naturalist' novels they wrote were in an extremely elaborate style enriched, as they thought, with exotic imagery and words from these artistic studies. This was the famous *écriture artiste*. This over-rich style is of course foreign to the genius of French, with its simplicity, clarity and logic. After his brother's death Edmond continued to write. He had a vitriolic pen and behaved like a serpent to his friends Flaubert, Zola, Daudet, Maupassant and others. The *Journal des Goncourt* is one of the most notorious and treacherous literary diaries in existence. Here Maupassant is retaliating after years of spiteful backbiting.

at the simplicity of their fellow writers. These will possibly hit the writers who have a body, but they will never hurt simplicity, which has not.

G. de M.

La Guillette, Étretat, September 1887

Pierre and Jean

Chapter 1

'Dash it!' old Roland suddenly exclaimed, after staying motionless for a quarter of an hour staring at the water and now and again gently lifting his line which had sunk into the depths.

Mme Roland, dozing in the stern beside Mme Rosémilly, a guest on this fishing expedition, woke up and turned to her husband:

'Well, well, what's up, Gérôme?'

The old boy snapped back in a temper:

'They're not biting at all now. I've caught nothing since twelve o'clock. You should only go fishing with men. Women always make you set out too late.'

His two sons, Pierre and Jean, one to port and the other to starboard, who each had a line twisted round a finger, both began laughing, and Jean answered back:

'You're not being very polite to our guest, Dad.'

M. Roland apologized in embarrassment:

'I beg your pardon, Mme Rosémilly, I'm like that. I invite ladies because I like their company, and then as soon as I get the feeling of water under me I think of nothing else but fish.'

Mme Roland was by now wide awake and looking sentimentally at the wide horizon of cliffs and sea. She murmured:

'And yet you've had a good catch.'

Her husband shook his head in disagreement, though he did at the same time glance with a complacent eye at the basket in which the fish caught by the three men were still wriggling feebly, with a tiny sound of slimy scales, flapping fins, weak, useless efforts and gasping in the deadly air.

Old Roland gripped the basket between his knees and tipped

it to make the silver stream of fish come up to the edge so that he could see the ones underneath, and their dying palpitations grew more intense, and the strong smell from their bodies, a healthy reek of the sea, rose from the full belly of the basket.

The old fisherman sniffed it eagerly, as one smells roses, and declared:

'Cripes! They're fresh, that lot!'

Then he went on:

'And how many did the doctor get?'

His elder son Pierre, a man of thirty with black side-whiskers cut like a magistrate's but otherwise clean-shaven, answered:

'Oh, not many, three or four.'

The father turned to the younger son:

'And you, Jean?'

Jean, a tall, fair young fellow with a full beard and much younger than his brother, smiled and murmured:

'Much the same as Pierre, four or five.'

They told the same fib every time, and it delighted old Roland.

He twisted his line round a rowlock, and folding his arms he announced:

'Never again shall I try to fish in the afternoon. Once you get past ten o'clock it's no use. The blighters don't bite any more, they take a siesta in the sun.'

The old boy surveyed the sea all round him with a smug proprietorial air.

He had been a jeweller in Paris, but an inordinate love of boating and fishing had dragged him away from his counter as soon as he had made enough to live modestly on his investments.

So he retired to Le Havre, bought a boat and became an amateur sailor. His two sons, Pierre and Jean, had stayed on in Paris to complete their studies, coming down from time to time to spend their holidays and share their father's pleasures.

After leaving school the elder son, Pierre, five years older than Jean, had felt a vocation for one profession after another and tried half a dozen, only to get sick of each one immediately and throw himself into new projects.

Finally medicine had attracted him and he had set to work with such enthusiasm that he had just qualified as a doctor after a quite short period of study and exemptions obtained from the Ministry. He was excitable, intelligent, volatile yet tenacious, full of utopian ideals and philosophical ideas.

Jean, as fair as his brother was dark, as calm as his brother was hasty, as equable as his brother was irritable, had serenely read law and passed his diploma at the same time as Pierre had qualified as a doctor.

So now they were both taking a little time off with the family, and both were planning to set themselves up in Le Havre if they could do so under satisfactory conditions.

But a vague jealousy, one of those dormant jealousies that develop between brothers or sisters almost unnoticed until maturity, only to burst out when one of them marries or has a stroke of good fortune, kept them constantly on the alert in a fraternal, unaggressive hostility. They did love each other, yet they kept an eye on each other. Pierre, five years old when Jean was born, had looked with the hostility of a spoilt little animal upon this other little animal that had suddenly appeared in his mother's and father's arms and was so loved and cherished by them.

From babyhood Jean had been a model of good behaviour, kind and equable, and Pierre had gradually become more and more impatient at hearing everlasting praises heaped on this big lump whose gentleness struck him as soft, his goodness as silly and his benevolence as lacking in perception. His parents were placid folk who dreamed of honourable, mediocre situations for their sons, and they criticized his indecisions and crazes, his schemes that came to nought, all his abortive aspirations towards noble ideas and distinguished professions.

Since he had reached man's estate he was no longer told: 'Look at Jean and imitate him!' But every time he heard them repeating: 'Jean has done this, Jean has done that,' he grasped the hidden meaning and the implication behind the words.

Their mother, a methodical woman, a slightly sentimental, middle-class housewife, a shopkeeper endowed with a tender soul, was constantly smoothing over the little rivalries that the trifling events of family life gave rise to day by day between her two big boys. Just at the moment, moreover, her peace of mind was disturbed by one little circumstance, and she was afraid of a complication. During the winter, while her boys were finishing their respective studies, she had made the acquaintance of a neighbour, Mme Rosémilly, widow of the captain of an ocean-going vessel who had died two years previously. The young widow, quite young, only twenty-three, a capable woman with an instinctive knowledge of life, like a free animal that has seen, experienced, understood and weighed every possible eventuality and judged it with a healthy, limited and kindly mind, had got into the habit of dropping in of an evening for a bit of needlework and talk over a cup of tea with these friendly neighbours.

Old Roland, always spurred on by his seafaring craze, used to question their new friend about the late captain, and she talked about him and his voyages and the tales he used to tell, without any embarrassment, for she was a reasonable and resigned woman fond of life but respectful of death.

When they came home the two sons, finding this pretty widow regularly about the place, had at once begun to pay court to her, not so much out of a desire to please her as a need to cut each other out.

Their mother, always prudent and practical, very much hoped that one of them would win, for the young lady was rich, but at the same time she did not want the other one to be hurt.

Mme Rosémilly was blonde, with blue eyes and a mop of unruly hair that blew about in the slightest wind, and she had something jaunty, bold and combative about her that did not fit in at all with the methodical prudence of her mind.

Already she seemed to prefer Jean, attracted towards him by

a similarity in their natures. But this preference was only betrayed by an almost imperceptible difference in voice and eyes, and moreover by the fact that she sometimes was influenced by his opinion.

She seemed to guess that Jean's opinion would reinforce her own, while that of Pierre was bound to be different. When she talked about the doctor's ideas, whether political, artistic, philosophical or moral, she would sometimes say: 'the bees in your bonnet.' At such times he would give her the cold stare of a magistrate building a case against women, all women, poor creatures!

Never before his sons' return had old Roland invited her to his fishing expeditions, to which he never took his wife either, for he loved to set off before daylight with Captain Beausire, retired captain of a liner, whom he had met in the harbour watching the boats come in and with whom he had become firm friends, and Papagris, an old salt nicknamed Jean-Bart, who looked after the boat.

Now, when one evening the previous week Mme Rosémilly had had dinner with them and said: 'It must be great fun fishing,' the ex-jeweller, whose passion was flattered and who was seized with a desire to communicate it and make new converts like a priest, had exlaimed:

'Do you want to come?'

'Yes, rather!'

'Next Tuesday?'

'All right, next Tuesday.'

'Are you the sort of woman who can set off at five in the morning?'

She uttered a cry of horror.

'Oh no, certainly not!'

He was disappointed and let down, and at once had his doubts about her vocation. All the same he asked:

'What time could you set off?'

'Well . . . at nine!'

'Not before?'

'No, not before, that's very early as it is!'

The old man hesitated. They would catch nothing for certain, because the fish stop biting as soon as the sun warms up, but the two brothers had eagerly undertaken to arrange the expedition and organize and settle everything there and then.

So the following Tuesday the *Perle* had dropped anchor under the white cliffs of Cap de la Hève, and they had fished there until noon, then taken a nap, then fished again, but caught nothing, and old Roland, realizing a bit late in the day that Mme Rosémilly was really only interested in and enjoying the trip on the water, and seeing, moreover, that his lines had given up twitching, he had let fly with his impatient 'Dash it!' which was addressed as much to the uninterested widow as to the uncatchable fish.

Now he was examining the catch, his catch, with the exultant joy of a miser, then he glanced up at the sky and noticed that the sun was going down.

'Well, my boys,' he said, 'suppose we do something about getting home?'

They both pulled in their lines, wound them up, cleaned the hooks, stuck them into corks and waited.

Roland stood up to survey the horizon, like a captain.

'The wind's dropped,' he said, 'you chaps 'll have to row.'

Then he suddenly pointed to the north and added:

'Oh look! The Southampton boat.'

In the direction he was pointing, above the calm sea which stretched out like an immense shiny blue cloth with glints of gold and flame, there rose a cloud, blackish against the pink sky. Beneath it they could make out the ship, looking very tiny from so far away.

Southwards other clouds of smoke could be seen, lots of them, all moving towards the jetty of Le Havre, which they could just make out as a white line, with the lighthouse jutting up at the end like a horn.

Roland asked:

'Isn't the *Normandie* due in today?'

'Yes, Dad,' answered Jean.

'Give me my glass, I think that's her over there.'

He pulled out the brass tube, adjusted it to his eye, looked for the place and suddenly exclaimed with delight at having seen it:

'Yes, yes, it's her, I recognize her two funnels. Would you like to have a look, Mme Rosémilly?'

She took the thing and pointed it towards the distant liner, but no doubt without being able to get it in position, for she couldn't make anything out, nothing but blue, with a ring of colour like a rainbow all round, and then weird shapes, like you see in an eclipse, that made her feel giddy.

As she gave back the telescope:

'Anyhow, I have never been able to use that instrument. It even used to annoy my husband, who spent hours at the window watching the ships go by.'

Old Roland was irritated, and went on:

'It must be to do with defective vision because my glass is excellent.'

Then he offered it to his wife:

'Want to look, dear?'

'No thanks, I know already that I couldn't see anything.'

Mme Roland, a woman of forty-eight but who didn't look it, seemed more than anyone else to be enjoying the trip and the close of day.

Her brown hair was only just beginning to turn grey. She looked placid and sensible, with an air of happiness and kindness that was a pleasure to see. As her son Pierre put it, she knew the value of money, but that didn't prevent her from indulging in the charm of dreams. She loved reading novels and poetry, not for their artistic value, but for the sake of the melancholy, tender reveries they called up in her. A line of poetry, often banal, often bad, would make a little cord vibrate, as she used to say, and give her the sensation of a mysterious desire almost realized. She enjoyed these gentle emotions which slightly disturbed a soul that was as well kept as an account-book.

Since settling in Le Havre she had visibly put on weight, and her formerly lithe and slender figure had become thicker.

This trip on the sea had thrilled her. Her husband was not malicious, but he did bully, though without anger or animosity, as do petty tyrants who think that giving orders means swearing. In front of any stranger he behaved himself, but in his family he let himself go and pretended to be terrible although he was really scared of everybody. She always gave in and asked for nothing because of her horror of noise, scenes and pointless explanations; so it had been a long time since she had asked Roland to take her out in the boat. Hence she had jumped at this chance, and she was savouring this rare new pleasure.

Since they had set out she had given herself up wholly, body and mind, to the gentle gliding over the water. She did not think, nor did she let her memories or hopes go wandering, but her heart seemed to her, like her body, to be floating on something downy, fluid and delicious that lulled her into semi-consciousness.

When Father gave the order to return: 'Come along, take your rowing positions!' she smiled as she saw her sons, her two big sons, take off their jackets and roll up their shirtsleeves, showing their bare arms.

Pierre, the one nearer the two women, took the bowside oar and Jean the stroke side, and they waited for the captain to shout 'Full speed ahead, all!' for he insisted that actions be carried out according to rule.

Together, as one man, they dipped their oars, then lay back, pulling with all their might, and a contest of strength began. They had come out quite easily with the sail, but the wind had dropped, and the male pride of the two brothers was suddenly aroused by the prospect of pitting their skill against each other.

When they went fishing alone with their father they rowed like that without anybody steering, for Roland prepared his lines while keeping an eye on the craft, which he steered with a gesture or word: 'Jean, ease off. You, Pierre, pull hard.' Or else he would say: 'Come on, number one, come on, number two, a bit of elbow grease.' Then the one who was dreaming would pull harder, the one who was pulling away would slack off, and the boat would get on course.

Today they were going to display their biceps. Pierre's arms were hairy, a bit thin but sinewy, Jean's plump and white, with a touch of pink and knotted muscles rippling under the skin.

At first Pierre had the advantage. Gritting his teeth, frowning, legs stretched out and hands gripping his oar, he made it bend along its whole length with each of his efforts, and the *Perle* veered towards the coast. Old Roland, seated in the bow so as to leave the whole of the back seat for the two women, burst his lungs shouting: 'Gently, number one, pull hard, number two.' But number one only redoubled his fury, and number two could not keep pace with this frenzied rowing.

Finally the boss ordered 'Stop!' The two oars rose together and on his father's orders Jean rowed alone for a few moments. But from then onwards he kept the advantage, got excited and warmed up, while Pierre, breathless and exhausted after his burst of energy, was weakening and puffing. Four times running old Roland called a halt to let his first-born get his breath and set the drifting boat back on course. Then the doctor, with sweat running down his face but his cheeks pale, humiliated and furious, muttered:

'I don't know what's come over me. A sort of stitch over the heart. I started off very well but it took the strength out of my arms.'

Jean asked: 'Would you like me to take both oars and row alone?'

'No thanks, it'll pass.'

His mother exclaimed in annoyance:

'Look here, Pierre, what's the sense in getting yourself into such a state, you're not a child, after all!'

He shrugged his shoulders and began rowing again.

Mme Rosémilly appeared not to see, understand or hear anything. With each movement of the boat her little fair head gave a pretty jerk backwards, lifting her fine hair off her temples.

But old Roland shouted: 'Look, there's the *Prince Albert* overhauling us.' They all looked. Long and low, with its two funnels raked backwards and its two yellow paddleboxes as round as cheeks, the Southampton boat was coming in at full speed, packed with passengers and open sunshades. Her quick, noisy paddles, beating the water that fell back in foam, made her look in a hurry, like a messenger in haste, and her straight bows cut through the sea, throwing up two narrow transparent waves that ran along her hull.

When she was near the *Perle*, Pa Roland raised his hat and the two women waved their handkerchiefs, and half a dozen sunshades waved vigorously in reply as the boat moved off, leaving a few gentle wavelets on the calm, gleaming surface.

Other vessels could be seen, similarly capped with smoke, heading from every direction towards the short, white jetty that swallowed them like a mouth, one after another. And fishing smacks and big sailing ships with delicate masts and spars shining against the sky, hauled by invisible tugs, were all coming in faster or slower towards this devouring ogre, who now and again seemed sated and vomited out into the open sea another fleet of liners, brigs, schooners and three-masters, their spars a thicket of tangled branches. Steamers hurried off to right and left over the flat belly of the ocean, while sailing ships, abandoned by the tugs that had towed them, stood motionless while donning from maintop to fore topgallant the white canvas or the brown that seemed red in the setting sun.

Mme Roland murmured with half-closed eyes:

'Heavens, how lovely the sea is!'

Mme Rosémilly replied with a long drawn-out but by no means sad sigh:

'Yes, but it can do a lot of harm sometimes.'

Roland exclaimed:

'Look! There's the *Normandie* waiting to go in. Isn't she enormous?'

Then he held forth about the coast opposite, right over there on the other side of the Seine estuary, twenty kilometres wide, he said. He pointed out Villerville, Trouville, Houlgate, Luc, Arromanches, the Caen river and the rocks of Calvados which are a danger to navigation all the way to Cherbourg. Then he went into the question of the Seine sandbanks that shift with every tide and fox even the pilots of Quillebœuf unless they go over the channel every day. He noted how Le Havre separated Lower from Upper Normandy. In Lower Normandy, pastures, meadows and fields come right down to the sea along the flat coast. The coast of Upper Normandy, on the other hand, is straight, being one great cliff carved out, indented and grand, making an immense white wall all the way to Dunkirk, every dent in which had a village or a port – Étretat, Fécamp, Saint-Valéry, Le Tréport, Dieppe, etc.

The two women were not listening, for they were in a state of happy torpor, thrilled by the view of the ocean covered with ships running about like animals round their lair, and they said nothing, rather awed by this vast expanse of water and sky and silenced by this comforting, magnificent sunset. Roland alone chattered on endlessly; he was one of those who are impervious to everything. Women, being more finely adjusted, sometimes sense, without understanding why, that the sound of a useless voice is as irritating as an obscenity.

Pierre and Jean had calmed down and were rowing slowly, and the *Perle*, heading for port, looked very tiny beside the great ships.

When she touched the quay the sailor Papagris was waiting, and he took the ladies' hands to help them ashore and they all dived into the town. Quite a big crowd, the crowd that goes down to the jetty every day at high tide, was quietly returning home too.

Mesdames Roland and Rosémilly went ahead, followed by the three men. On the way up the rue de Paris they stopped from time to time at a dress shop or a jeweller's to look at a hat or a piece of jewellery, then went on after exchanging opinions.

At the place de la Bourse Roland surveyed, as he did every

49

day, the commercial harbour, full of shipping which over-flowed into other basins, in which the huge hulls, belly to belly, were touching each other four or five deep. All the numberless masts along several kilometres of quays, with their yards, mastheads and cordage, made this open space in the middle of the town look like a great dead forest. Above this leafless forest the gulls wheeled round and round with an eye to any garbage thrown into the water, on which they would swoop down like a falling stone, and a boy fixing a pulley to the end of a main-royal looked as if he had climbed up there bird-nesting.

'Will you have dinner with us – no formality – so as to finish the day together?' Mme Roland asked Mme Rosémilly.

'Yes, I'd love to, and I accept with no formality either. It would be miserable to go home all alone this evening.'

Pierre, who had overheard, and whom the lady's indifference was beginning to vex, muttered: 'Here we go, the widow's digging herself in now.' For some days he had been calling her the widow. Although this term did not signify anything it irritated Jean simply by the way it was said, which he thought nasty and hurtful.

The three men did not say another word until they were on their own doorstep. It was a narrow house, with a ground floor and two little floors above, in the rue Belle-Normande. The maid Joséphine, a lass of nineteen, a peasant servant on the cheap, exceedingly well endowed with the yokel's astonished and cowlike look, opened the door, shut it again and followed her employers up the stairs to the parlour on the first floor, then said:

'Some gentleman come three times.'

Pa Roland, who never addressed her without bawling and swearing, shouted:

'Who came, for God's sake?'

She never let the master's shouting put her off, so went on:

'A gent from the lawyer's.'

'What lawyer?'

'M. Canu, of course.'

'And what did the gentleman say?'

'That M. Canu will come himself during the evening.'

Maître Lecanu was the lawyer and to some extent a friend of old Roland, whose affairs he managed. It must be something urgent and important for him to give notice of a visit that evening, and the four Rolands looked at each other, upset by this news as people of modest means always are when a lawyer comes on the scene, conjuring up all sorts of ideas about contracts, legacies and lawsuits, things desirable or frightening. After a few seconds of silence the father murmured:

'Now whatever can this be about?'

Mme Rosémilly began to laugh:

'Well of course, it's a legacy, I'm sure of it! I bring good luck.'

But they were not hoping for the death of anyone who might leave them anything.

Mme Roland, gifted with an excellent memory for family connections, at once began going into all the marriages on her husband's side and her own, following out people's children and working out ramifications.

Before she even took off her hat she asked:

'I say, Father' — (she always called her husband Father at home, and sometimes Monsieur Roland in front of strangers) — 'I say, Father, do you remember who was the second wife of Joseph Lebru?'

'Yes, a Duménil girl, daughter of a stationer.'

'Any children by her?'

'I should think so, four or five at least.'

'No, nothing from that quarter then.'

She was already warming up to the hunt and fastening on to this hope of a bit of money dropping from the sky. But Pierre, who was very fond of his mother and knew she sometimes went in for daydreaming, was afraid of a disillusionment and a bit of grief and even distress if the news turned out to be bad instead of good. So he stopped her.

Don't get carried away, Mother, no American uncles nowadays! I should think it might be about a wife for Jean.'

Everybody was surprised at this idea, and Jean was a bit narked that his brother had talked like that in front of Mme Rosémilly.

'Why me rather than you? It's a very unlikely supposition. You're the eldest, so they would have thought of you first. And besides, I don't want to get married.'

Pierre scoffed:

'Are you in love, then?'

The other was annoyed and answered:

'Is it necessary to be in love to say you don't want to get married just yet?'

'Oh of course, the "yet" explains everything. You're waiting.'

'All right, say I'm waiting if you like.'

But old Roland, who had been listening and reflecting, suddenly hit on the most likely solution.

'Why, of course, how silly we are to rack our brains! M. Lecanu is a friend of ours, he knows that Pierre is looking out for a medical practice and Jean for a legal one, and he has found something to suit one of you.'

It was so simple and probable that they all agreed.

'It's all ready,' announced the maid.

They all went to their rooms to wash their hands before sitting down.

Ten minutes later they were having dinner in the little dining-room on the ground floor. At first there was scarcely any conversation but after a few moments Roland was again amazed at the clerk's visit.

'Anyhow, why didn't he write, why send his clerk three times, why not come himself?'

Pierre thought it was quite natural.

'He probably wants an immediate answer, and perhaps he has some confidential clauses that are better not put in writing.'

Nevertheless they all stayed preoccupied, and all four were a little put out at having invited this stranger who would cramp their discussions about the decisions to be taken.

They had just gone back upstairs to the parlour when the lawyer was announced.

Roland rushed at him.

'Good evening, Maître.'

He gave M. Lecanu the title *Maître* which precedes the name of every notary.

Mme Rosémilly stood up.

'I'm off, I'm very tired.'

There were feeble attempts to make her stay, but she refused and went off, with none of the three men taking her home as somebody always did.

Mme Roland fussed over the newcomer.

'A cup of coffee, Monsieur?'

'No thanks, I've come straight from dinner.'

'Well, a cup of tea, then?'

'I won't say no, but a bit later, we'll talk business first.'

In the deep silence following these words nothing could be heard except the regular tick of the clock, and downstairs the noise of the washing-up being done by the maid, who was too stupid even to listen at keyholes.

The lawyer went on:

'When you were in Paris did you know a certain M. Maréchal, Léon Maréchal?'

M. and Mme Roland uttered the same exclamation:

'I should think we did!'

'He was a friend of yours?'

'Our best, Monsieur,' said Roland, 'but an incurable Parisian who won't leave the boulevard. He is a principal clerk in the finance department. I've not seen him since I left the capital. And now we don't write any more. You know how it is when you live at a distance from each other . . .'

The lawyer went on solemnly:

'M. Maréchal is deceased.'

Man and wife made simultaneously that little gesture of

sad surprise, whether genuine or put on, with which one receives such news.

M. Lecanu continued:

'My colleague in Paris has just informed me of the main provision of his will whereby he names your son Jean, M. Jean Roland, as his residuary legatee.'

So great was the amazement that nobody could find a word to say.

Mme Roland was the first to control her emotion. She stammered:

'Oh dear, poor Léon . . . our poor friend . . . oh dear, oh dear . . . dead!'

Her eyes filled with tears, the silent tears of women, drops of sorrow from the soul that run down the cheeks and look so painful because they are so transparent.

However, Roland was not thinking so much of the sadness of this loss as of the hope it gave. But he did not dare to ask questions immediately about the clauses of the will and the amount of the fortune, and so, by way of working towards the interesting question, he asked:

'What did poor Maréchal die of?'

M. Lecanu had no idea.

'I only know,' he said, 'that having passed away without direct heirs, he leaves his entire fortune, an income of some twenty thousand francs in 3 per cent debentures, to your second son, whom he saw born and watched grow up and whom he thinks worthy of this legacy. In the event of non-acceptance on M. Jean's part, the money would go to a foundling hospital.'

Already Pa Roland could not conceal his joy and he exclaimed:

'Good Lord, that is a kind thought straight from the heart. Now if I had been without an heir I wouldn't have forgotten him either, such a good friend!'

The lawyer smiled.

'It has made me so happy to tell you this myself. It has always been a pleasure to bring good news to people.'

It had not occurred to him at all that this good news was the death of a friend, and old Roland's best friend at that, and Roland himself had suddenly forgotten this attachment he had advertised so convincingly just before.

Only Mme Roland and her sons kept sad expressions. She was still crying a little, dabbing her eyes with her handkerchief, which she then put over her mouth to stifle her heavy sighs.

The doctor murmured:

'He was a kind man and very fond of us. He often had my brother and me to dinner.'

Jean's eyes were wide open and shining, as with a familiar movement he took his fine fair beard in his right hand and smoothed it down to the last hairs as though trying to make it longer and thinner.

Twice he moved his lips to make some suitable remark too, and after much thought all he could find was this:

'Yes, he really was very fond of me, and always kissed me when I went to see him.'

But the old man's thoughts were racing on, running round this legacy they had been informed about, money that was already theirs, lurking behind the door and about to come in quite soon, tomorrow, on a formal word of acceptance.

He asked:

'Are there any possible snags? No lawsuits? No matters in dispute?'

M. Lecanu seemed quite untroubled.

'No, my Paris colleague assures me that the situation is quite straightforward. All that is required is M. Jean's acceptance.'

'Excellent . . . and the estate is quite unencumbered?'

'Perfectly.'

'All the formalities have been complied with?'

'Yes, all.'

Suddenly the ex-jeweller felt slightly ashamed, with a vague, instinctive and momentary shame at his haste to find out, so he went on:

'You do realize that my asking you all these things straight away is so as to save my son a lot of unpleasantness he might not foresee. Sometimes there are debts or an involved situation, or something of that sort, and you get yourself into an inextricable thicket. However, I'm not the one who is inheriting, but I'm thinking of the little chap first.'

In the family they always called Jean the little chap, although he was much bigger than Pierre.

All of a sudden Mme Roland seemed to be emerging from a dream and to be recalling some far-off thing, something almost forgotten that she had heard some time but was not quite sure about, and she murmured:

'Weren't you saying that poor dear Maréchal left his money to my little Jean?'

'Yes, Madame.'

She went on quite simply:

'That gives me great pleasure, for it proves he loved us.'

Roland was now on his feet.

'Would you like my son to sign his acceptance at once, dear Maître?'

'No, no, M. Roland. Tomorrow, tomorrow at my office at two o'clock, if that suits you.'

'Oh yes, oh yes indeed!'

Mme Roland had stood up too, and was smiling through her tears. She took two steps towards the lawyer, placed her hand on the back of an armchair, and casting upon him the affectionate eyes of a grateful mother, asked:

'And what about that cup of tea, Monsieur Lecanu?'

'Yes please, Madame, I should love it now.'

The girl was summoned and first brought in some *gâteaux-secs* in deep tins, those tasteless and tooth-breaking English confections apparently baked for parrot's beaks and soldered into tins for journeys round the world.* Then she went to

*The words are untranslatable ('dry cakes' is nonsense) and the things, in spite of what Maupassant says, have never been seen in England. They have the consistency of hard sugar icing and about as much taste. A

fetch some grey-looking napkins, folded into little squares, those tea-napkins never washed in thrifty households. She came back a third time with the sugar-basin and cups, then went off to boil the water. Then they waited.

Nobody could say a word, they had too much to think about and nothing to say. Only Mme Roland tried to think of some trivial remarks. She mentioned the fishing expedition, sang the praises of the *Perle* and of Mme Rosémilly.

'Charming, charming,' the lawyer said at intervals.

Roland, with his back against the marble chimneypiece as though it were winter and the fire burning, hands in pockets and lips moving in a whistling position, could not keep still and was tortured by an uncontrollable desire to let all his joy burst forth.

The two brothers, sitting in two similar armchairs, with their legs crossed in the same way, on either side of the table in the middle, were staring in front of them in attitudes similar but expressing different emotions.

At last the tea appeared. The lawyer took his cup, sugared it and drank it, after crumbling into it a little cake too hard to bite, then he rose, shook hands all round and left.

'Right-oh,' repeated Roland, 'tomorrow at your office at two.'

'Right, tomorrow at two.'

Jean had not said a word.

After the lawyer had gone there was another silence, then Roland walked over and clapped his open hands on his younger son's shoulders, exclaiming:

'Well, you lucky devil, aren't you going to give me a kiss?'

That made Jean smile and he kissed his father and said:

'That didn't strike me as indispensable.'

But the old chap couldn't contain himself for joy. He walked up and down, played the piano on the furniture with his clumsy nails, pivoted on his heels and said over and over again:

typical example of the universal tendency to attribute anything unpleasant or obscene to a foreign country.

'What luck! What luck! This really is a stroke of luck!'

Pierre asked:

'So you must have known this Maréchal very well in those days?'

His father answered:

'I should think so, he spent every evening with us. But surely you remember how he picked you up at school when you had a day's holiday and often took you back after dinner. Why of course, it was he who went for the doctor on the morning Jean was born! He had had a meal with us when your mother felt the pains. We realized at once what it was and he rushed off. In his haste he took my hat instead of his own. I remember that because later on we had a good laugh about it. It is even probable that he remembered that detail at the time of his death, and as he had no heir he said to himself: "Well, as I helped at the birth of that youngster I'll leave him my money!"'

Mme Roland, deep in an armchair, seemed to be lost in memories. As though thinking aloud she said:

'Oh, he was a good friend, very devoted, very faithful, a kind of man rare in these times!'

Jean stood up.

'I'm going for a little walk,' he said.

His father was surprised and wanted to keep him at home because they had things to discuss, plans to make, decisions to take. But the young man insisted, and invented an appointment. After all, they would have plenty of time to decide things before they got possession of the legacy.

So off he went, for he wanted to be alone to think. Pierre said he was going out too, and followed his brother a few minutes later.

As soon as he was alone with his wife Roland seized her in his arms, kissed her ten times on each cheek, and by way of answering a criticism she had often made:

'So you see, dear, that there wouldn't have been much point in my staying any longer in Paris, slaving for the children instead of coming here to regain my health, since this fortune has dropped on us from the skies.'

She had become very grave.

'It drops from the skies for Jean, but what about Pierre?'

'Pierre? But he's a doctor, he'll earn plenty of money . . . and besides, his brother will certainly do something for him.'

'No. He'd never accept it. And besides, this legacy is Jean's, and only Jean's. So Pierre is very much at a disadvantage.'

The old boy seemed puzzled.

'Well, we'll leave him a bit more in our wills.'

'No, that isn't very fair either.'

He exploded:

'Well, what the hell! What do you expect me to do about it? You are always on the look-out for nasty ideas! You have to spoil all my enjoyment. Well, I'm off to bed. Good night. All the same it's a bit of luck, a damn good bit of luck!'

He went off, delighted in spite of all and with never a word of regret for the friend who had been so generous in his hour of death.

Mme Roland fell back into her dreams in the light of the smoking lamp.

Chapter 2

As soon as he was outside, Pierre made for the rue de Paris, the main street of Le Havre, brightly lit, busy and noisy. The fresh air from the sea caressed his face, and he walked along slowly, his stick under his arm and hands behind his back.

He felt ill at ease, listless and miserable as people do when they have had some upsetting news. He was not distressed by any particular idea, and he could not have found a reason at first for this heaviness of spirit and numbness of body. He felt a pain somewhere but could not say where. There was within him some little place that hurt, one of those almost imperceptible bruises that cannot be located, yet fidget, tire, depress and irritate you, an unidentifiable, trifling pain, a sort of seed of unhappiness.

When he reached the place du Théâtre he was attracted by the lights of the Café Tortoni and strolled over to the brilliantly lit windows, but as he was about to go in it occurred to him that he would find friends and acquaintances there, people he would have to talk to, and he felt a sudden distaste for the boring mateyness of cups of coffee and tots of spirits. So he retraced his steps and went back along the main street leading to the harbour.

He wondered where he might go and tried to think of some place he would like that would appeal to his mood. He couldn't think of one, for being alone got on his nerves, yet he wouldn't have wanted to meet anyone.

Having reached the main quay he hesitated once more, then turned towards the jetty. He had opted for solitude.

As he passed close to a seat on the breakwater he sat down, tired already and sick of his walk before he had finished it.

He asked himself what was the matter with him that evening, and began hunting in his memory for some setback that had affected him, as one questions a patient to find the reason for his temperature.

He had a mind that was both excitable and wary at the same time, he flew out of control but then reasoned and either approved of his outbursts or censured them, but his first instincts also had the last word, and the emotional man always dominated the intelligent one.

So he tried to find the reason for the jangled state he was in, this need for movement but desire for nothing, this urge to meet somebody for the sake of differing from him and also this distaste for the people he might meet and the things they might say.

Then he asked himself this question: 'Would it be Jean's inheritance?'

Yes, that was possible after all. When the lawyer announced the news he had felt his heart beat a little faster. Of course you aren't always able to master your own feelings and you experience spontaneous and persistent emotions against which you struggle in vain.

He began musing deeply on this physiological problem of the impression produced by some event upon the instinctive man, which generates in him a current of ideas and painful or enjoyable sensations running contrary to those desired, called into play and considered good and healthy by the thinking man who, by cultivating his intelligence, has become superior to himself.

He endeavoured to visualize the state of mind of the son who inherits a large fortune thanks to which he is about to enjoy many pleasures he has coveted for a long time but been denied by the niggardliness of a father whom nevertheless he loved and mourned.

He stood up and resumed his walk to the end of the jetty. He felt better, pleased to have understood, to have caught himself by surprise and uncovered the other man who inhabits each one of us.

'So I have been jealous of Jean,' he thought. 'That's really pretty low! I'm sure of it now, for the first thing that came into my mind was his marriage to Mme Rosémilly. Yet I am not in love with that priggish little silly, who is perfectly designed to sicken anybody of good sense and prudence. So this is gratuitous jealousy, the very essence of jealousy, which exists simply because it exists! This wants watching.'

He came to the signal post that indicates the depth of water in the harbour, and he struck a match to read the list of ships reported in the roadstead and due to come in on the next tide. Liners were expected from Brazil, the River Plate, Chile and Japan, also two Danish brigs, a Norwegian schooner and a Turkish steamer, which surprised Pierre as much as if he had read 'a Swiss liner'; and he saw in a sort of weird dream a great vessel swarming with men in turbans climbing into the rigging in baggy trousers.

'How stupid,' he thought, 'for after all the Turks are a maritime people.'

A few steps further on he stopped to look out at the roadstead. To his right, above Sainte-Adresse, the two electric beacons on Cap de la Hève, like two gigantic twin Cyclopes, threw their long powerful beams across the sea. Starting from the two adjacent lamps, the two parallel rays, like the gigantic tails of two comets, dropped down a straight and immeasurable slope from the highest point on the coast to the furthest horizon. Then two other lights on the two jetties, children of these giants, marked the harbour entrance; and far off across the Seine yet others could be seen, lots of others, fixed or winking, with either blinding flashes or darkness, opening and shutting like eyes, the eyes of the seaports, yellow, red, green, watching the dark sea covered with ships, the living eyes of the welcoming land saying, just by the mechanical, invariable, regular movement of their lids: 'It's me, I'm Trouville, I'm Honfleur, I'm the river of Pont-Audemer.' And dominating all the others, so high in the sky that from such a distance it could be taken for a planet, the aerial light of Étouville showed the way to Rouen through the sandbanks of the estuary of the great river.

Then over the deep water of the limitless sea, blacker than the sky, you thought you could see a star here and there. They twinkled in the misty night, far or near, white, green and red too. Nearly all of them were stationary, but one or two seemed to be moving. These were the lights of vessels at anchor waiting for the next tide or vessels in motion coming in to find an anchorage.

Just at that moment the moon rose behind the town, and she looked like the huge, divine light set in the firmament to guide the vast fleet of real stars.

Pierre murmured almost aloud:

'Look at that, and we get worked up about potty little sums of money!'

Suddenly close by him, in the broad black trench between the jetties, a shadow, a great fantastic shadow, glided along. Leaning over the granite parapet, he saw a fishing boat coming home, without any sound of voice or wave or oar, gently propelled by its lofty brown sail set to catch the breeze from the sea.

He thought: 'If one could live on that how peaceful it would be, perhaps.' Then after a few more steps he saw a man sitting at the end of the mole.

A dreamer, a lover, a wise man, someone happy or sad? Who was it? He went up, curious to see the face of this solitary man, and he recognized his brother.

'Oh, it's you, Jean.'

'Oh, hallo Pierre . . . What have you come here for?'

'Just to take the air. What about you?'

Jean began to laugh.

'I'm taking the air too.'

Pierre sat down by his brother.

'Isn't it just beautiful!'

'Oh yes.'

By his tone of voice Pierre realized that Jean hadn't looked at anything. He went on:

'Whenever I come here I have a mad desire to go away, sail

away with all these ships, north or south. Just think, all those little lights have come from all corners of the earth, countries with huge flowers and lovely girls, pale or copper-coloured, the lands of humming-birds, elephants, lions at large, black kings, all the countries that are fairy-tales for us now that we don't believe any more in the White Cat or the Sleeping Beauty. Wouldn't it be grand to be able to take a trip somewhere like that. But there you are, you need money, lots of it...'

He stopped short as the thought came to him that his brother had this money now, and that being free of all worry, with no hindrances, happy and gay, he could go wherever he thought good, to the golden-haired Swedish girls or the dark girls of Havana.

Then a thought ran through his mind, one of those involuntary thoughts so frequent with him and that came so suddenly that he could neither foresee them nor check or modify them, that seemed to come from another independent and violent personality: 'What the hell! He's too silly, he'll marry that little Rosémilly woman.'

He got up.

'I'll leave you to dream about the future, I want to go on walking.'

He shook his brother's hand and went on in the friendliest tone:

'Well, young Jean, so you're rich! I am so glad to have run into you alone tonight to say what pleasure this gives me, how much I congratulate you and love you.'

Jean, with his gentle, affectionate nature, was deeply moved and stammered out:

'Thanks... thanks, you're a good sort, Pierre, thank you.'

Pierre wandered off slowly, stick under arm, hands behind him.

Back in the town he asked himself over and over again what he was going to do, and was vexed at this interrupted walk and having been done out of the sea by his brother's presence.

He had an inspiration: 'I'll go up and have a drink

with old Marowsko,' and made for the Ingouville district.

He had met old Marowsko in the Paris hospitals. He was an elderly Pole, a political refugee, it was said, who had had some terrible adventures in that country and had come to practise his calling of pharmacist in France after taking fresh examinations. Nobody knew anything about his past life and so tales had run around among the housemen and medical students and later among the neighbours. This reputation of being a terrible conspirator, a nihilist, a regicide, a patriot ready for anything, who had miraculously escaped death, had fired the lively and daring imagination of Pierre Roland, and he had become friendly with the old chap, but without ever having had from him any admission about his former existence. Moreover it was thanks to the young doctor that the Pole had come to settle in Le Havre, counting on the numerous clientele that the new doctor would send to him.

Meanwhile he was living humbly in his modest chemist's shop, selling medicines to the small tradesmen and working-class people in the neighbourhood.

Pierre often went to see him before dinner for an hour's talk, for he liked the calm face and spasmodic conversation of Marowsko, whose long silences struck him as profound.

A single gas-jet was burning above the counter which was covered with bottles. To save money those in the window had not been lit. Behind the counter, sitting on a chair with his legs stretched out one on the other, fast asleep with his chin on his chest, was a bald old man with a great beak of a nose which, coming straight down from his hairless forehead, made him look like a gloomy parrot.

At the tinkle of the bell he woke up, jumped to his feet and, recognizing the doctor, came forward to meet him with outstretched hands.

His black frock-coat, streaked with stains of acids and syrups and much too big for his skinny little body, looked like an ancient cassock, and the man spoke with a marked Polish accent which gave his high-pitched voice something childish, with the lisps and intonations of a little thing beginning to talk.

Pierre sat down and Marowsko asked:

'Any fresh news, doctor?'

'Nothing. Always the same everywhere.'

'You don't seem very cheerful this evening.'

'I'm not often very cheerful.'

'Now, now, you must shake that off. Have a drop of liqueur?'

'Thanks, I'd love to.'

'Well, now, I'm going to make you taste a new concoction. For a couple of months I've been trying to make something out of red currants, which so far have only been used for cordial. Well, I've done it! I've done it! A good liqueur, very good indeed.'

Full of delight he went to a cupboard, opened it, found a bottle and brought it over. His comings and goings and actions were all done in tentative movements, never complete ones, he never stretched his arm right out or opened his legs wide, never made any full or definite movement. His ideas seemed like his actions, he indicated them, foreshadowed them, sketched them, suggested but never stated them fully.

Moreover his great interest in life seemed to be the preparation of cordials and liqueurs. 'With a good cordial or a good liqueur you can make a fortune,' he often said.

He had invented hundreds of sugary preparations without succeeding in putting one on the market. Pierre used to say that Marowsko reminded him of Marat.

Two liqueur glasses were found in the back parlour and brought in on the mixing-board; then the two men examined the colour of the liquid by holding it up to the gas.

'A lovely ruby!' declared Pierre.

'Yes, isn't it?'

The Pole's ancient parrot-head looked delighted.

The doctor tasted, savoured, thought awhile, tasted again, thought again and made a pronouncement:

'Very good, very good and quite a new flavour. A discovery, my friend!'

'Oh really? I'm so glad.'

Then Marowsko sought advice about baptizing the new liqueur. He wanted to call it 'essence of currant', or 'currant fino', or 'currantia', or perhaps 'currantette'.

Pierre didn't approve of any of these names.

Then the old boy had an idea:

'What you said just now is very good: "Lovely Ruby".'

The doctor questioned the value of this name too, although he had thought of it, and he simply advised 'currantine', which Marowsko declared admirable.

Then they fell silent and sat there in the gaslight for some minutes without a word.

At length, and almost in spite of himself, Pierre came out with:

'A rather strange thing happened to us this evening. A friend of my father's has died and left his fortune to my brother.'

The chemist didn't seem to understand at first, but after some thought he said that he hoped the doctor would inherit half. When the matter had been properly explained, he seemed vexed and surprised, and to express his displeasure at seeing his young friend cut out, he repeated several times:

'That won't look too good.'

Pierre, whose agitation was coming on again, wanted to know what Marowsko meant by this phrase.

Why shouldn't it look too good? What ill effects could come from his brother's inheriting the fortune of a friend of the family?

But the old man was wary and offered no further explanation.

'In a case like this the money is left to the two brothers equally. I tell you, it won't look too good.'

Exasperated, the doctor went off to the parental home and went to bed.

For some time he could hear Jean walking softly up and down in the next room, then, after drinking two glasses of water, he went to sleep.

Chapter 3

HE woke next day with a firm resolve to make a fortune.

He had already made this resolve several times without following it up in real life. At the outset of all these attempts at a new career, the hope of getting rich quickly had buoyed up his efforts and confidence until the first obstacle, the first setback, which had switched him on to a new track.

So, snug in his bed between the warm sheets, he meditated. How many doctors had become millionaires in a short time! You only needed a grain of professional know-how, for in the course of his studies he had been able to sum up the most celebrated professors and had decided they were donkeys. He was certainly as good as them, if not better. If he managed somehow to secure the rich and elegant Le Havre clientele he could make a hundred thousand francs a year easily. Indeed he worked out with precision the certain profits. In the mornings he would go out visiting patients. Taking as an average, and quite a modest one, ten per day at twenty francs each, that would give a minimum of 72,000 francs a year, or even 75,000, for the figure of ten patients was lower than it would certainly be. In the afternoons he would have another average of ten patients visiting him at ten francs, say 36,000 francs. That made 120,000 in round figures. Old patients and friends he would visit at ten francs, or have call on him at five, which would probably lower this figure slightly, but that would be made up by consultations with other doctors and all the little regular perquisites of the profession.

Nothing simpler than to reach that position with some skilful publicity – news items in the *Figaro* about how the Parisian scientific establishment had its eye on him, how interested it was in some amazing cures brought off by the obscure young doctor in Le Havre. And then he would be richer than his brother, richer and more famous and contented with himself because he would owe his fortune to himself alone, and he would show his generosity to his aged parents, justly proud of his fame. He would not marry, not wanting to hamper his existence with one troublesome woman, but he would select mistresses from among his prettiest patients.

He felt so sure of success that he leaped out of bed as if to seize it there and then, and he dressed to go and look round the town for the flat that would suit him.

As he wandered through the streets he considered how trivial are the causes determining our acts. For three weeks past he could have, indeed should have, taken this decision which no doubt had suddenly been born within him as a result of his brother's inheritance.

He stopped in front of doors displaying a notice about a beautiful flat or a luxury flat to let; notices without any adjective always left him full of scorn. Then he inspected them with a haughty air, measuring the height of ceilings, drawing a plan of the place in his notebook, the doors and passages, the position of the doors to the outer world, making it plain that he was a doctor and had many callers. The staircase must be wide and kept clean, and in any case he could not go higher than the first floor.

Having taken note of seven or eight addresses and jotted down some two hundred bits of information, he got home for lunch a quarter of an hour late.

As soon as he was in the hall he heard a sound of plates. So they had started without him. Why? They were never as punctual as that in the house. He felt hurt and annoyed, for he was rather touchy. As he went in his father said:

'Come on, Pierre, make haste, dammit! You know we're going to the lawyer's at two. This isn't a day for dawdling about.'

The doctor sat down without answering, after kissing his

mother and shaking hands with his father and brother, and took the cutlet saved for him from the dish in the middle of the table. It was cold and dried up. It would certainly be the nastiest. He thought they might have left it in the oven until he came in, and not have lost their heads to the extent of forgetting their other son, the elder son, completely. The conversation was taken up again at the point where he had interrupted it.

'If I were you,' Mme Roland said to Jean, 'this is what I'd do at once. I would set myself up expensively, so as to catch people's eye, be seen in society, ride a horse and choose one or two interesting cases so as to defend them and get well thought of at the Courts. I would like to be a sort of amateur barrister much in demand. God be praised, you are now free of care, and if you take up a profession it is really so as not to throw away the benefit of your studies and because a man must never just do nothing.'

Old Roland declared, in the middle of peeling a pear:

'Good Lord, if I were in your shoes I'd buy a fine boat, a cutter like our pilot boats, and I'd go all the way to Senegal in it.'

It was Pierre's turn to give his advice. What it boiled down to was that it wasn't a man's fortune that established his moral value or intellectual worth. For mediocrities money only brought degeneration, while on the other hand it put a powerful tool into the hands of the strong. And there weren't many of these, be it noted. If Jean really was a superior sort of man he could show it now he was free from want. But he would have to work a hundred times harder than he would have done in other circumstances. It was not a case of pleading for or against the widow and the orphan and pocketing so much for each case won or lost, but of becoming an eminent lawyer, a beacon of justice.

He added by way of conclusion:

'If I had money I wouldn't half dissect some bodies!'

Old Roland shrugged.

'Tra-la-la! The wisest thing in life is to take it easy. We aren't beasts of burden but men. When you're born poor you have to work. All right, you have to work and lump it. But when you have an income – good heavens, you must be a mug to work yourself to death.'

Pierre answered loftily:

'Our ideas are not the same! For my part the only things in the world I respect are knowledge and intelligence, everything else is beneath contempt.'

Mme Roland constantly tried to soften the effects of the incessant collisions between father and son, so she changed the subject and talked about a murder committed the week before at Bolbec-Nointot. Everybody's mind was immediately occupied by the circumstances of the crime and thrilled by the interesting horror, the absorbing mystery of crimes which, even if commonplace, shameful and revolting, cast a strange and universal spell over human curiosity.

Now and again, however, old Roland pulled out his watch:

'Come along, we must be starting.'

Pierre was scornful.

'It isn't one o'clock yet. Really it wasn't necessary to make me eat a cold chop.'

'Are you coming to the lawyer's?' asked his mother.

He snapped back: 'Me? No, what for? My presence is quite pointless.'

Jean stayed silent as though this was nothing to do with him. When they were discussing the murder at Bolbec he had, as a lawyer, expressed a few ideas and developed a few opinions about crimes and criminals. Now he was silent again, but the brightness of his eyes and the healthy pink of his cheeks, even the glossiness of his beard seemed to proclaim his happiness.

When the family had gone Pierre, alone again, resumed his investigations into flats to let. After two or three hours of tramping up and down staircases he eventually discovered something nice on the boulevard François I, a big mezzanine with two entrances on different streets, two reception rooms and a glassed-in gallery in which patients while waiting their turn could walk up and down surrounded by flowers, and a delightful circular dining-room with a view over the sea.

As he was on the point of renting it the figure of 3,000 francs stopped him, for the first quarter had to be paid in advance and he had nothing, not a penny in sight.

The modest capital saved by his father yielded barely 8,000 francs per year, and Pierre reproached himself for having often caused his parents financial worry by his long hesitations about choosing a career, his false starts and continual embarkings on fresh courses of study. So he left with a promise to decide within two days, and it did occur to him to ask his brother for this first quarter, or even the half-year, 1,500 francs, as soon as Jean came into his money.

'It will be a loan for hardly more than a few months,' he thought. 'Perhaps I shall even pay it back before the end of the year. It's quite simple, and besides, he'll be glad to do this for me.'

As it was not yet four and he had nothing, absolutely nothing, to do, he went and sat in the Park, and he stayed there a long time on a seat without an idea in his head, staring at the ground, overcome with a weariness that was really quite painful.

And yet every day since he had been back home he had lived like this and never suffered so cruelly from the emptiness of life and his own inaction. How had he passed the time between getting up and going to bed?

He had hung about on the jetty at high tide, hung about in the streets, hung about in cafés, at Marowsko's, everywhere. And now all of a sudden this life, quite bearable so far, was becoming hateful, intolerable. If he had had any money he could have hired a carriage and gone for a long drive in the country, beside farm ditches shaded by beeches and elms, but he had to count the cost of half a pint or a postage stamp, and such daydreams were not for him. He suddenly thought how hard it is, at past thirty, to have to come down to asking his mother for a louis from time to time and blush while doing so. Scratching the ground with his stick he murmured:

'Curse it! If only I had some money!'

And the thought of his brother's legacy entered his flesh once again like a wasp-sting, but he impatiently thrust it aside, not wanting to let himself slip down the slope of jealousy.

There were some children round him playing in the dust on the paths. They had long fair hair, and with very earnest faces and solemn attention were making little mountains of sand so as to stamp on them and squash them underfoot.

Pierre was going through one of those gloomy days when one looks into every corner of one's soul and shakes out every crease.

'Our occupations are like the work of those kids,' he thought. Then he wondered whether after all the wisest course in life was not to beget two or three of these little useless beings and watch them grow with complacent curiosity. And he was touched by the desire to marry. You aren't so lost when you're not alone any more. At any rate you can hear somebody moving near you in times of worry and uncertainty, and it is something anyway to be able to say words of love to a woman when you are feeling down.

He began thinking about women.

His knowledge of them was very limited, as all he had had in the Latin Quarter was affairs of a fortnight or so, dropped when the month's money ran out and picked up again or replaced the following month. Yet kind, gentle, consoling creatures must exist. Hadn't his own mother brought sweet reasonableness and charm to his father's home? How he would have loved to meet a woman, a real woman!

He leaped up, determined to go and pay a little visit to Mme Rosémilly.

But he quickly sat down again. No, he didn't like that one! Why not? She had too much dull, boring common sense, and besides, didn't she seem to prefer Jean? Without his clearly admitting it to himself, this preference had a good deal to do with his low opinion of the widow's intelligence, for although he loved his brother he could not help thinking him rather ordinary and himself rather superior.

But he couldn't stay there all day, and as on the previous evening he anxiously asked himself, 'What am I going to do?'

He felt in his soul a thirst for affection, a need to be fondled and consoled. Consoled for what? He couldn't have said, but he was at one of those times of weakness and lassitude when a woman's presence, a woman's caress, the touch of a hand, the rustle of a dress and a soft look from brown or blue eyes seem to be immediately necessary to our hearts.

Then he remembered a little barmaid he had gone home with one night and seen once or twice since.

So he got up once again to go and have a drink with this girl. What would he say to her? And she to him? Nothing, perhaps. What did that matter? He would hold her hand for a few moments! She seemed to be keen on him, so why didn't he see her more often?

He found her dozing on a chair in the almost empty bar. Three customers were smoking their pipes, their elbows propped on the oak tables, the cashier was reading a novel, while the landlord in his shirtsleeves was fast asleep on the bench.

As soon as she saw him the girl jumped up and came over to him.

'Hallo, how are you?'

'Not too bad, how's yourself?'

'Oh, I'm all right. Don't see you very often!'

'No, I don't get much time to myself. You know I'm a doctor.'

'Oh really? You never told me. If I'd known when I was ill last week I'd have consulted you. Well, what'll you have?'

'Half a pint. And you?'

'Same for me, as you're paying, dear.'

74

And she went on 'dearing' him as if his standing her this drink had been tacit permission. Then they chatted, sitting face to face. Now and again she held his hand with the easy familiarity of girls whose caresses are for sale, and looking at him with alluring eyes she said:

'Why don't you come more often, dear? I'm very fond of you, darling.'

But he was getting sick of her already, deciding that she was silly, common, typically low-class. Women, he told himself, should be seen in a dream or surrounded by an aura of luxury to romanticize their vulgarity.

She asked:

'The other morning you went past with a good-looking fair man with a full beard. Is he your brother?'

'Yes, that's my brother.'

'He's a jolly handsome man!'

'Do you think so?'

'Oh yes, and he looks like a chap who enjoys life.'

What strange urge suddenly made him tell this barmaid about Jean's inheritance? Why should this subject, which he thrust away from him when he was alone, and repelled for fear of the distress it brought to his soul, why should it rise to his lips at that moment, and why did he let it escape, as though he needed once again to empty out the overflowing bitterness of his heart to somebody?

Crossing his legs, he said:

'He isn't half lucky, that brother of mine, he's just inherited an income of twenty thousand francs.'

She opened wide her blue and greedy eyes.

'Oh! And who left him that? His granny or some aunt?'

'No, an old friend of my parents.'

'Only a friend? Not possible! And he hasn't left you anything?'

'No, I didn't know him very well.'

After a few moments' thought she said with a funny smile:

'Well, your brother's lucky to have friends like that. It's

75

not surprising he looks so unlike you, and that's a fact!'

He felt like boxing her ears without quite knowing why, and asked her, tight-lipped:

'What do you mean by that?'

She put on a silly and simple air.

'Oh nothing. I mean he's luckier than you are.'

He threw a franc on the table and went out.

But now he kept on repeating to himself: 'It's not surprising he looks so unlike you.'

What had she thought and what had she been suggesting by these words? There was certainly something malicious, spiteful and infamous in them. Yes, that girl must have thought that Jean was Maréchal's son.

The emotion he felt when he thought of this suspicion cast on his mother was so violent that he stopped short and looked round for somewhere to sit down.

There was another café opposite, and he went in, sat on a chair, the waiter came and he asked for a half.

His heart was banging and shivers were running over his skin. Then suddenly he called to mind what Marowsko had said the day before: 'That won't look too good.' Had the same thought occurred to him, the same suspicion as had struck this tart?

As he leaned over his beer studying the white froth fizzing and dispersing, he asked himself: 'Is it possible for people to believe such a thing?'

The reasons why this odious doubt should come to people's minds now appeared one after another, and they were clear, obvious and infuriating. That an old bachelor with no heir should leave his money to the two children of a friend – nothing simpler or more natural. But that he should give it in its entirety to one of those children would certainly surprise people, make them whisper and finally smile. Why hadn't he foreseen that, why hadn't his father felt it and why hadn't his mother guessed it? No, they had been too delighted with this unexpected money for such an idea to enter their heads.

76

And besides, how could these decent people have suspected such a shameful thing?

But wouldn't the outer world, the neighbours, the shop-keepers and the tradesmen, in fact all the people who knew them, repeat this abominable thing, see the funny side of it, gloat over it, laugh at his father and despise his mother?

The observation made by the barmaid that Jean was fair and he was dark, that they did not resemble each other in face, walk, build or intelligence, would now strike the eye and the mind of everybody. When people referred to one of the Roland sons they would say: 'Which one, the genuine or the fake?'

He got up resolved to warn his brother and put him on his guard against the awful threat to their mother's honour. But what would Jean do? The simplest thing, obviously, would be to refuse to accept the legacy, which would then go to the poor, and merely tell friends and acquaintances who knew all about the bequest that it contained unacceptable clauses and conditions that would have made Jean not an heir but a trustee.

On his way home he thought he had better see his brother alone about it, so as not to raise such a subject in front of his parents.

But as he opened the door he heard a loud noise of voices and laughter in the drawing-room, and on going in he heard Mme Rosémilly and Beausire, who had been brought home by his father and were being kept to dinner to celebrate the great news.

Vermouth and absinthe had been served to give them an appetite, and they had all got themselves into a jolly mood. Captain Beausire, a short, round man, round through having rolled over the seven seas, whose ideas seemed round, too, like pebbles on the shore, and who laughed with his throat full of r's, considered life an excellent thing in which everything was there for the taking.

He was raising his glass to old Roland while Jean was giving the ladies second glasses.

Mme Rosémilly was by way of refusing when Captain Beausire, who had known her late husband, exclaimed:

'Come, come, Madame, *bis repetita placent*, as we say in the vernacular, which means: "A couple of vermouths never did anybody any harm." Now look at me, since I gave up the sea I give the boat a few artificial rollings like this every day before dinner time! I add a slight pitching after the coffee, and that gives me a heavy sea for the evening. I never go as far as a tempest, mind you, never, never, because I'm afraid of sustaining damage.'

Roland, whose nautical mania was flattered by the old sea-dog, was laughing his head off, already red in the face, his eyes bleary with absinthe. He had a big shopkeeper's belly, and nothing but a belly, into which the rest of his body seemed to have retreated, one of those soft bellies belonging to wholly sedentary men, who have no thighs, chest, arms or neck left, the seat of their chair having concentrated all their substance into the same place.

Beausire, on the other hand, although short and fat, looked as solid as an egg and hard as a bullet.

Mme Roland had not yet finished her first glass, and pink with happiness, her eyes shining, she was contemplating her son Jean.

With him joy was now freely bursting forth. The thing was signed and settled, he had twenty thousand a year. By the way he laughed, his louder voice when he talked, the way he looked at people, his more forthright manner and greater assurance, you could sense the confidence that comes with money.

Dinner was announced, and as old Roland was about to offer his arm to Mme Rosémilly: 'No, no,' cried his wife, 'today everything is for Jean.'

The table was resplendent with a quite unusual luxury. In front of Jean's place, next to his father's, there rose, like a dome decked with flags, an enormous bouquet full of silk favours, a really ceremonial bouquet, and it was flanked by four fruit dishes, one of which contained a pyramid of magnificent peaches, the second a monumental gâteau covered with whipped cream and icing-sugar bells, in fact a pastry cathedral, the third slices of pineapple swimming in clear syrup, and the fourth (unheard-of luxury) black grapes from warmer climes.

'Golly!' said Pierre as he sat down, 'we are celebrating the accession of Jean the Rich.'

After the soup Madeira was served, and already everybody was talking at once. Beausire was recounting a tale about a dinner he had had at San Domingo as guest of a Negro general. Old Roland was listening and trying to slip in between the sentences another tale about another dinner given by one of his friends at Meudon, as a result of which every one of them had been ill for a fortnight. Mme Rosémilly, Jean and his mother were working out a plan for an outing and lunch at Saint-Jouin that they already thought would give them immense pleasure, while Pierre wished he had eaten alone in some eating-house by the sea and avoided all this noise, laughter and joy that was getting on his nerves.

He wondered how he was now going to set about telling his brother his fears and make him give up the fortune he had already accepted, which he was enjoying and already finding intoxicating. It would be hard for him, of course, but it had to be; he couldn't hesitate, for the reputation of their mother was in danger.

The entry of an enormous bass sent Roland back into fishing stories. Beausire told some amazing ones about Gaboon, Sainte-Marie in Madagascar and above all off the coasts of China and Japan, where the fish have faces as funny as the inhabitants. Then he held forth about those fishes' faces, their big golden eyes, blue or red bellies, strange fins like fans, tails cut out like crescent moons, and he acted it all in such a killing way that all the listeners laughed till they cried.

Pierre alone seemed incredulous and murmured: 'It's quite true to say that the Normans are the Gascons of the north!'

After the fish came a vol-au-vent, then a roast chicken,

79

salad, runner beans and a Pithiviers lark pâté. Mme Rosémilly's maid was helping with the serving, and the gaiety went on growing with the number of glasses of wine. When the first champagne cork popped, old Roland, very excited, imitated the sound of this detonation with his mouth, then declared:

'I prefer that to a pistol shot!'

Pierre, who was getting more and more irritated, answered with a sneer:

'But that is probably more dangerous for you!'

Roland, about to drink, put his full glass down on the table and asked:

'Why, pray?'

For a long time he had been complaining about his health, of headaches, giddy turns and constant inexplicable discomforts. The doctor went on:

'Because the pistol shot may well miss you, but the glass of wine is bound to go down into your stomach.'

'Well, what then?'

'Well, then it burns up your stomach, upsets your nervous system, impedes your circulation and prepares the way for the apoplexy that threatens all men of your constitution.'

The ex-jeweller's growing tipsiness appeared to have blown away like smoke in the wind, and he turned anxious and staring eyes upon his son, trying to make sure that he was not joking.

But Beausire exclaimed:

'Oh, these blessed doctors, they're all the same: don't eat, don't drink, don't make love, cut out all fun and games. It's all naughty-naughty for your poor little health. Well, Sir, I've gone in for all that in every part of the world, wherever I could and as much as I could, and I'm none the worse for it!'

Pierre observed tartly:

'In the first place, Captain, you are stronger than my father, and then all self-indulgent people talk like you until the day when ... And they don't come back the day after to say to the prudent doctor: "Doctor, you were right." When I see my father doing the worst and most dangerous things for him it's natural that I should warn him. I should be a bad son if I did anything else.'

Terribly upset, Mme Roland intervened:

'Really, Pierre, what's the matter with you? It won't hurt him just for once. Remember what a special occasion this is for him and all of us. You'll spoil all his pleasure and make us all miserable. You're being very nasty!'

He shrugged his shoulders and murmured:

'He can do as he likes, I've warned him.'

But old Roland didn't drink. He looked at his glass full of golden, luminous wine, whose soul, light and intoxicating, was breaking forth, rising from the bottom in tiny bubbles thick and fast and bursting on the surface. His expression had the wariness of a fox coming upon a dead chicken and suspecting a trap.

He ventured to ask:

'Do you think it would do me a lot of harm?'

Pierre felt remorseful and blamed himself for making other people suffer because of his ill-humour.

'No, no, it's all right for just once, drink away. But don't overdo it and get into a habit.'

Thereupon old Roland raised his glass, but still didn't decide to put it to his lips. He studied it mournfully, with mingled desire and fear, then he sniffed at it, tasted it and took little sips, savouring them, but his heart was full of anguish, weakness and greed, and then regrets as soon as he had consumed the last drop.

Suddenly Pierre caught Mme Rosémilly's eye, fixed on him, limpid and blue but comprehending and hard. He felt or read or guessed the angry thought in the mind of this little woman, with her simple straightforward nature, for her eyes said: 'You are jealous, and that's shameful!'

He lowered his eyes and went on with his meal.

He was not hungry and thought everything was nasty. He was tormented by a desire to get away, a desire not to be among these people or hear them talk, joke and laugh any more.

By now old Roland, beginning to be troubled again by the fumes of wine, was already forgetting his son's advice and casting sidelong, loving glances at a bottle of champagne beside his plate and still almost full. He dared not touch it for fear of a fresh lecture, and was wondering what trick or sleight of hand he could employ so as to get it without incurring fresh remarks from Pierre. He thought of a ruse, and the easiest of all: he nonchalantly picked up the bottle, and holding it near the bottom stretched out across the table to refill the doctor's glass first, then he went round the other glasses, and when he reached his own he began talking very loud, and if he did pour something into it you would certainly have sworn it was done inadvertently. In fact nobody took any notice.

Without thinking what he was doing, Pierre was drinking a great deal. He was jumpy and irritable, and every minute he unconsciously picked up and put to his lips the long crystal glass in which the bubbles rose through the sparkling, transparent liquid. Then he poured it very slowly into his mouth so as to feel the little sweet pricking sensation of the gas as it evaporated on his tongue.

Gradually a pleasant warmth ran through his body. It began in his stomach, which seemed to be the source of heat, reached his chest, invaded his limbs and spread throughout his flesh like a warm, health-giving wave carrying joy along with it. He felt better, not so impatient or annoyed, and his resolve to speak to his brother that very night weakened, not because the thought of giving it up altogether occurred to him, but in order not to upset so soon the sense of well-being he was experiencing.

Beausire rose to propose a toast.

After bowing all round he spoke:

'Most gracious ladies and gentlemen, we are gathered here to celebrate a joyful event which has befallen one of our friends. It was said in olden times that Fortune was blind, but I think she was just short-sighted or mischievous, and that she has bought an excellent pair of marine binoculars which has enabled her to pick out in the port of Le Havre the son of our good friend Roland, captain of the *Perle*.'

Bravos burst from all mouths, supported by clapping, and Roland senior rose to reply.

After coughing, for his throat seemed to need clearing and his tongue felt heavy, he managed to falter:

'Thank you, Captain, thank you on my own behalf and that of my son. I shall never forget how you have acted in these circumstances. Here's wishing you everything you wish for yourself.'

His eyes and nose were full of tears, and he sat down again, finding nothing else to say.

Jean was laughing as he took the floor in his turn.

'I am the one,' he said, 'who should at this point thank the devoted friends, the excellent friends (looking at Mme Rosémilly) who are today giving me this touching proof of their affection. But it is not merely in words that I can express my gratitude. I will prove it tomorrow, at every moment of my life, always, for our friendship is not one of the transitory kind.'

His mother, deeply moved, murmured:

'Well done, my boy.'

But Beausire exclaimed:

'Come along, Mme Rosémilly, you must speak for the fair sex.'

She raised her glass and in a sweet voice, slightly tinged with sadness, said:

'I drink to the blessed memory of M. Maréchal.'

There were a few seconds of quietness and fitting meditation, as after a prayer, and then Beausire, who was fertile in compliments, remarked:

'Only women can think of such delicacy.'

Then turning to Roland senior:

'What was M. Maréchal really like? Were you all very intimate with him?'

The old boy, sentimental in his cups, burst into tears and mumbled:

'A brother . . . you know . . . the kind you never find again . . . we were always together . . . he had dinner with us every evening . . . he took us out for little treats at the theatre . . . that's all I can say . . . that's all . . . all. A friend, a true . . . a true . . . er, wasn't he, Louise?'

His wife merely said:

'Yes, he was a faithful friend.'

Pierre watched his father and mother, but as the conversation turned to something else, he fell to drinking again.

He hardly remembered anything about the rest of the evening. They had had coffee, a few liqueurs, and there had been a lot of laughing and joking. Then he went to bed at about midnight, with his mind in a whirl and his head aching. He slept like a log until nine the following morning.

Chapter 4

PERHAPS this slumber, bathed in champagne and chartreuse, had softened and calmed him, for he woke up feeling very kindly disposed. While dressing he assessed, weighed and summed up his emotions of the previous day, trying to sift out clearly and completely the real, secret, personal causes as well as the external ones.

It might well have been that the barmaid had thought the worst, a real whore's notion, when she heard that only one of the Roland sons had inherited from an unknown man; but then don't creatures like that always have such utterly groundless suspicions about all decent women? Every time they open their mouths don't you hear them abusing, slandering and destroying the reputation of any women they feel are above reproach? Every time anyone mentions in front of them the name of some blameless person they take umbrage, as though they are being insulted, and exclaim: 'Ah, but you see, dear, I know these married women, they're a nice lot! They've got more lovers than us, only they keep them hidden because they are hypocrites. Oh yes! A nice lot, they are!'

On any other occasion he would certainly have failed to understand, let alone have supposed possible, any such insinuations about his poor mother, who was so good, so simple, so worthy of respect. But his soul was troubled by this leaven of jealousy fermenting within him. His over-tense mind, on the look-out, as it were, in spite of himself, for anything that could hurt his brother, might even have credited that barmaid with odious intentions she had never had. It might well have been that his imagination alone, which he could not control and which was constantly dodging his will-power and sallying forth free, bold, adventurous and full of guile into the boundless universe of ideas, whence it sometimes returned with un-mentionable, shameful ones that it kept locked inside him, in the unfathomable depths of his soul like stolen goods – it might well have been that this imagination alone had created and invented this horrible doubt. It must be that his own heart had its secrets hidden from him, and that wounded heart must have found in this abominable doubt a means of depriving his brother of the inheritance he coveted. He suspected himself now, and as the ultra-religious do with their consciences, he questioned all the mysteries of his own thoughts.

Of course, for all her limited intelligence, Mme Rosémilly had the tact, flair and subtle instinct of women. Yet this idea had not occurred to her, for she had drunk in perfect good faith to the blessed memory of Maréchal. She would not have done so had she harboured the slightest suspicion. Now he felt quite sure; his involuntary dissatisfaction at the fortune that had fallen upon his brother, and also certainly his quasi-religious love for his mother, had sharpened his scruples, pious and praiseworthy scruples, but exaggerated.

As he came to this conclusion he felt happy at once, as one does when a good deed has been done, and he resolved to show himself pleasant to everybody, beginning with his father, whose crazes, silly statements, commonplace opinions and all-too-visible mediocrity constantly got on his nerves.

He did not get home late for lunch and amused the whole family by his wit and high spirits.

His mother was delighted, and said:

'Dear Pierre, you've no idea how comic and witty you are when you want to be.'

And he chattered on, found comic phrases and made them laugh at ingenious portraits of their friends. Beausire was a good target, and Mme Rosémilly to a lesser degree, but discreetly and without too much malice. As he looked at his brother he thought: 'But why don't you stand up for her, you ninny. You may well be rich, but I shall always cut you out when I want to.'

Over coffee he said to his father:

'Are you using the *Perle* today?'

'No, son.'

'Can I take her with Jean-Bart?'

'Yes of course, for as long as you like.'

He bought a cigar at the first tobacconist's he came to and strode gaily down to the harbour.

He looked at the clear, luminous sky, pale blue, refreshed and cleansed by the sea breeze.

The sailor Papagris, alias Jean-Bart, was dozing in the bottom of the boat he had to keep ready to sail any day at noon when they hadn't gone fishing in the morning.

'Just the two of us, boss!' Pierre called.

He went down the iron ladder from the quay and leaped into the craft.

'What's the wind?' he asked.

'Still blowing upstream, M'sieu Pierre. I got a good breeze out there.'

'All right, Dad, off we go.'

They hoisted the mizzen, weighed anchor and the boat, set free, began to glide slowly towards the jetty over the calm water of the harbour. The slight breath of air blowing from the streets caught the upper part of the sail so gently that nothing could be felt, and the *Perle* seemed to be animated with a life of her own, the life of ships, and borne ahead by a mysterious force hidden within her. Pierre had taken the tiller and, chewing his cigar, legs stretched out on the bench, eyes half closed in the dazzling rays of the sun, he watched the great tarred timbers of the breakwater as they passed near him.

When they came out into the open sea, reaching the tip of the northern jetty that had sheltered them, the breeze freshened up and ran over the doctor's face and hands like a cool caress and then down into his lungs which opened in a long sigh to drink it in, and, filling the brown sail and bellying it out, tilted the *Perle* and made her more responsive.

Jean-Bart at once hauled up the jib, and its triangle full of wind looked like a wing; then, gaining the stern in a couple of strides, he untied the jigger which was lashed to its mast.

Along the side of the hull, as the boat suddenly keeled over on to its side and sailed at full speed, there began a gentle but crisp sound of bubbling, running water.

The bow split open the sea like the blade of a runaway plough, and the uplifted wave, bending over and white with foam, curled round and fell back like the heavy brown earth of a ploughed field.

With each wave – they were small and close together – a shudder ran through the *Perle* from the jib to the rudder, which jerked in Pierre's hand. When the wind blew stronger for a few moments, the waves licked the gunwale as though about to invade the boat. A collier from Liverpool was at anchor waiting for the tide; they passed round its stern, then had a good look at the ships in the roadstead one after another, and finally moved further out to follow the coastline.

For three hours Pierre wandered over the moving waters, feeling peaceful, calm and happy as he controlled this thing of wood and cloth like a swift and docile winged beast which went hither and thither at his will, obeying the pressure of his fingers.

He let his dreams run on, as one does on horseback or on the deck of a ship, thinking about his future, which would be bright, and the pleasure of living intelligently. The very next day he would ask his brother to lend him 1500 francs for three months, so that he could move at once into that attractive flat on the boulevard François I.

Suddenly the sailor said:

'Fog coming up, M'sieu Pierre, we must get back.'

He looked up and saw to the north a grey shadow, dense but insubstantial, filling the sky and covering the sea, hurrying towards them like a cloud that had dropped from the heavens.

He turned about and with a following wind made for the jetty, pursued by the scurrying fog that was catching up fast. When it reached the *Perle*, blanketing it with its intangible thickness, a cold shiver ran over Pierre's limbs, and a smell of smoke and damp, that strange smell of sea fogs, made him shut his mouth so as not to taste the damp, freezing vapour. By the time the boat reached its usual mooring in the harbour the whole town was already shrouded in this light vapour that, though it did not actually fall, wetted everything like rain and flowed over houses and streets like a river.

Pierre hurried home, with his feet and hands frozen, and threw himself on to his bed to sleep until dinner-time.

As he went into the dining-room his mother was saying to Jean:

'The gallery will be lovely. We can put flowers there. You'll see. I'll take on looking after them and replacing them. When you give parties it will look just like fairyland!'

'What are you talking about?' asked the doctor.

'A lovely flat I've just rented for your brother. A real find, a mezzanine facing on to two streets. It has two reception rooms and a glassed-in gallery, a little circular dining-room, quite charming for a bachelor.'

Pierre changed colour. Anger gripped his heart.

'Where is this?'

'In the boulevard François I.'

Then he was sure, and sat down so enraged that he felt like shouting: 'This is too much! Isn't there anything for anyone except him?'

His mother, still radiant, went on talking away:

'And just fancy, I got it for 2,800 francs. They were asking 3,000, but I got 200 off by making an agreement for three, six or nine years. Your brother will be perfectly suited there. All a lawyer needs for making his fortune is an elegant home. It attracts the client, delights him, keeps him, inspires respect and makes him realize that a man living in such a style can get good fees for his pronouncements.'

She paused for a few seconds, then went on:

'We shall have to find something similar for you, much more modest because you've no money, but quite nice all the same. It would be very useful for you, believe me.'

Pierre answered scornfully:

'Oh, I shall make my way through work and skill.'

His mother insisted:

'Yes, but I assure you that a nice home would be very helpful all the same.'

About half-way through the meal he suddenly asked:

'How did you get to know this Maréchal?'

Old Roland looked up and rummaged in his memory.

'Just a minute, I don't quite remember now. It's such a long time ago. Oh yes, I know. Your mother got to know him in the shop – that's right, isn't it, Louise? He had been in to order something, and then he often came back. We knew him as a customer before we knew him as a friend.'

Pierre, who was eating some beans and stabbing them one by one with a prong of his fork as though he were running them through, went on:

'At what sort of time did this friendship begin?'

Roland thought again, but as he couldn't recollect anything more he called upon his wife's memory:

'Let me see, what year was it, Louise? You can't have forgotten because you have such a good memory. Let me see, it was in . . . er . . . '55 or '56? Try and think, you should know better than me.'

She did think for a few moments and then asserted quietly and with certainty:

'It was in '58, dear. Pierre was three years old then. I'm sure I'm not making a mistake because that was the year when the child had scarlet fever, and Maréchal, whom we didn't know very well at that stage, was a great help to us.'

Roland exclaimed:

'That's true, that's true, he really was wonderful! As your mother was worn out and I was busy in the shop, he used to go to the chemist's to get your medicine. He was a fine chap, and that's a fact! And when you had got over it you can't imagine how glad he was and how he kissed you. It was from then on that we became great friends.'

The sudden, devastating thought went into Pierre's soul like a bullet piercing through the flesh: 'As he knew me first and was so devoted to me, as he loved me and kissed me so much, as I am the cause of his great attachment to my parents, why has he left all his money to my brother and nothing to me?'

He asked no more questions and sat glum, absorbed rather than thinking, harbouring a new and so far vague worry, the hidden germ of a new malady.

He went out quite soon and began prowling round the streets again. They were shrouded in the fog that made the night heavy, opaque and nauseating. It was like a pestilential vapour over all the earth. He could see it going past the street lamps and sometimes it seemed to put them out. The paving stones were getting as slippery as on frosty nights, and all the bad smells seemed to be issuing from the bowels of the houses, stinks from cellars, gutters, drains, slum kitchens, and to be mingling with the horrible reek of this shifting fog.

With shoulders hunched and hands in pockets, Pierre made for Marowsko's, for he didn't want to stay out of doors in this cold.

Beneath the gas jet that kept watch for him the old chemist was asleep as usual. Recognizing Pierre, whom he loved with the love of a faithful dog, he shook off his torpor, went and found two glasses and brought the 'currantine'.

'Well,' asked the doctor, 'how far have you got with your liqueur?'

The Pole explained how four of the biggest cafés in the town agreed to launch it, and the *Phare de la Côte* and the *Sémaphore Havrais* would advertise it in exchange for some pharmaceutical products being made available to the staff.

After a long silence Marowsko asked if Jean was definitely in possession of his fortune, and then put one or two vague questions on the same subject. His jealous devotion to Pierre was shocked by this favouritism. And by the way his eyes avoided his, and the hesitant tone of his voice, Pierre believed he could read the chemist's thoughts, and guessed, understood and read the phrases rising to his lips which he didn't say, and wouldn't say because he was so prudent, timid and cautious.

Now he felt quite sure that the old man was thinking:

'You shouldn't have let him accept this legacy, which will give rise to talk about your mother.' Perhaps he even believed that Jean was Maréchal's son. Yes, he certainly did! How could he not believe it, for the thing must seem to him to be feasible, probable, obvious? But he himself, Pierre, the son, hadn't he been fighting for three days with all his might and with all the subtle arguments of his heart to deceive reason, fighting against this horrible suspicion?

Once again the need to be alone, to think, argue the thing out with himself in order to look at this possible but outrageous fact boldly, without scruples or weakness, possessed him so exclusively that he stood up without even drinking his glass of 'currantine', shook hands with the astonished chemist and plunged back into the foggy street.

He kept on saying to himself: 'Why has this Maréchal left all his money to Jean?'

It was no longer jealousy that made him seek an answer, nor the rather unworthy but natural envy he knew was hidden inside him and that he had been fighting against for three days, but terror of an appalling thing, terror of believing that his brother Jean was the son of this man!

No, he didn't believe it, he couldn't even ask himself this dastardly question. Yet he must reject totally and for ever this suspicion, however slight and improbable. He must have light and certainty, he must have complete security in his heart, for his mother was all he loved in the world.

Alone, wandering about in the night, he set about a minute inquiry into his own memory and reason from which the undeniable truth would emerge. After that it would be over and he would never think about it again, never. He would go and sleep.

His thoughts ran: 'Now let's examine the facts, then I'll recall everything I know about him, his behaviour with my brother and me, and go into all the causes which might have inspired this preference . . . He was present at Jean's birth? Yes, but he knew me before that. If he had loved my mother with a silent and undeclared love I'm the one he would have preferred because it was thanks to me and my scarlet fever that he became a close friend of my parents. So logically he should have chosen me and had a stronger affection for me, unless he had felt an instinctive attraction and preference as he watched my brother grow up.'

So he searched in his memory, with a desperate concentration of his whole mind and intellectual power, to reconstruct, see again, recognize and get to the heart of the man, this man who had been so near him but to whom he had meant so little all through his years in Paris.

But he felt that the act of walking, the gentle movement of his steps, muddled his ideas a bit, disturbed their concentration, limited their range, obscured his memory.

In order to look at the past and unknown events with acute vision that nothing could escape, he must be at rest in some vast and empty place. So he decided to go and sit on the harbour arm as he had the other night.

As he neared the harbour he heard out to sea a mournful, sinister plaint, like the bellowing of a bull, but longer drawn out and more powerful. It was the wail of a siren, the wail of ships lost in the fog.

A shiver ran through his flesh and froze his heart, for this cry of distress had so reverberated in his soul and nerves that he felt he had uttered it himself. Another similar voice wailed in its turn, further away, and then, right next to him, the harbour fog-horn answered them with a deafening blare.

Pierre walked faster and reached the jetty, thinking of

nothing now, content to enter this lugubrious, moaning darkness.

Seated at the far end of the mole he shut his eyes so as not to see the electric lamps, veiled in mist, marking access to the port by night, nor the red lamp of the lighthouse on the south jetty, scarcely distinguishable in any case. Then half turning, he put his elbows on the granite and buried his face in his hands.

His thoughts, though he never pronounced the word with his lips, constantly repeated: 'Maréchal! Maréchal!' as though summoning him, calling up and rousing his shade. In the blackness of his closed eyes he suddenly saw him as he used to know him. He was a man of sixty with a white beard trimmed to a point and bushy eyebrows, white as well. Neither tall nor short, he had a kindly look, and his soft grey eyes and gentle movements made him a thoroughly nice person, simple and affectionate. He used to call Pierre and Jean 'my dear boys', never seemed to prefer one to the other and had them both to dinner.

With the tenacity of a hound that has lost the scent Pierre began trying to recall words, gestures, intonations and facial expressions of this man who had vanished from the world. Little by little he rediscovered him, the whole of him, in his flat in the rue Tronchet when he invited his brother and himself to meals.

Two servants looked after him, both elderly women, and they had long got into the habit of saying 'Monsieur Pierre' and 'Monsieur Jean'.

Maréchal held out both hands to them, the right to one, the left to the other, just as they came.

They would chatter in a quiet, friendly way about ordinary things. Nothing exceptional about the man's mind, but he was most agreeable, charming and gracious. Certainly he was a good friend to them, one of those good friends you don't think much about because you feel they are utterly reliable.

Now memories were crowding back into Pierre's mind. On several occasions, seeing him preoccupied and guessing that as

94

a student he had money worries, Maréchal had offered and lent him money, quite unasked, a few hundred francs, perhaps, which had been forgotten on both sides and never repaid. Therefore the man always loved him and took an interest, since he was concerned about his needs. So . . . so why leave all his money to Jean? No, he had never been visibly more affectionate towards the younger than the elder, more concerned, less apparently fond of one than the other. So . . . so he must have had a powerful, secret reason for giving everything to Jean – everything – and nothing to Pierre.

The more he thought about it and lived over the past years again, the more he felt this distinction made between them to be unlikely, unbelievable.

Acute suffering and inexpressible anguish in his breast made his heart beat wildly like a bit of rag at the mercy of the wind. Its springs seemed broken and the blood coursed freely through, tossing and turning it uncontrollably.

Then, half to himself, like a man talking in a nightmare, he murmured: 'I must know. My God, I must know!'

And now he explored still further back, right into the earlier times when his parents lived in Paris. But the faces escaped him, and that confused his memories. Above all he struggled to recollect Maréchal – was his hair fair, brown or black? He couldn't do so because the latest face of this man, an elderly man's face, had effaced the others. But he did remember that he was slimmer, that his hands were soft and that he often brought flowers, very often, for his father was constantly saying: 'What, more bouquets? But my dear man, it's madness, you'll ruin yourself over roses!'

And Maréchal would answer: 'Never mind, it gives me pleasure.'

And suddenly the tone of voice of his mother, his own mother, smiling and saying: 'Thank you, my dear,' came back into his mind as clearly as if he could hear it now. Yes, she must have pronounced those four words very often for them to be etched like this on her son's memory.

So Maréchal, the rich man, the customer, used to bring flowers to the little woman in the shop, wife of his humble jeweller. Had he been her lover? How could he have become the friend of these shopkeepers if he hadn't loved the wife? He was a well-educated man with a very cultivated mind. How often had he talked to Pierre about poets and poetry? He didn't consider writers from an artist's point of view, but as an ordinary man with strong emotional responses. The doctor had often smiled at these moments of deep emotion, which struck him as a bit childish. Now he realized that this senti-mental man could never, never have been a friend of his father's, for his father was so literal, so down to earth and so dull that for him the very word poetry meant silliness.

So this man Maréchal, young, free, rich and open to any affection, had one day gone into a shop on the off-chance, hav-ing probably noticed the pretty woman behind the counter. He had bought something, come back, got into conversation, become more friendly each time, paying with frequent pur-chases for the right to come into this home and sit down, smile at the wife and shake the husband's hand.

And then later . . . later . . . Oh God, what had happened later?

He had loved and fondled the first child, the jeweller's child, until the birth of the next one, then he had remained inscrutable until death; and then, when his tomb was sealed, his flesh de-cayed, his name effaced from among the living, his whole being gone for ever, having nothing further to be careful about, noth-ing to fear or hide, he had given all his fortune to the second child. Why? This man was intelligent, he must have realized and foreseen that he might, indeed that he would almost inevit-ably, lead people to assume that this child was his. So he was casting dishonour upon a woman? How could he have acted thus unless Jean was indeed his son?

Suddenly a clear and dreadful memory pierced his very soul. Maréchal was fair, fair like Jean. He now recalled a little miniature portrait he had seen in the old Paris days on the sitting-room mantelpiece, and which had now disappeared. Where was it? Lost or hidden? Oh, if he could get hold of it, if only for a second! Perhaps his mother had kept it in the secret drawer where tokens of a bygone love are hidden away.

At this thought his distress became so agonizing that he groaned aloud. It was one of those short protests forced out of one's throat by excessive pain. And straightway, as though it had heard, understood and answered, the siren on the jetty roared out just by him. Its monstrous, supernatural clamour, more resounding than thunder, a savage, formidable roar intended to dominate the voices of wind and wave, spread out into the darkness and over the invisible sea, buried beneath the fog.

Then through the mists, from far and near, came similar cries in the night. And terrible they were, these cries for help from the great blinded ships.

Then it all relapsed into silence.

Pierre had opened his eyes and looked. He was surprised to be there, awake after his nightmare.

'I'm mad,' he thought, 'I'm suspecting my own mother.' A wave of love and affection, repentance, prayer and desolation swept over his heart. His own mother! Knowing her as he did, how could he have suspected her? Were not the soul and the life of this simple, chaste, faithful woman as clear as water? When you had seen and known her, how could you fail to rank her above suspicion? And he, her son, had had doubts about her! Oh, if he could have taken her there and then into his arms, how he would have embraced and caressed her, and knelt to beg forgiveness!

Could she have deceived his father, she of all people? His father! He was a good man, of course, honourable and straight-forward in business dealings, but a man whose mind had never ventured beyond the horizon of his shop. How could this woman, who had been very pretty, he knew, and indeed still was, and endowed with a delicate, affectionate and sensitive soul, how could she have accepted as her fiancé and husband a man so different from herself?

Why try to find out? She had got married as girls do marry the young man with some money introduced by their families. They had at once taken up their abode in their shop in the rue Montmartre, and the young wife, presiding at her counter, enthusiastic about her new home, and inspired by that subtle, sacred instinct for the common cause that takes the place of love and even affection in most shopkeeping couples in Paris, had set herself to work with all her active and discriminating intelligence to build up the fortune their business hoped to make. And so her life had gone on, uneventful, quiet, respectable, without love!

Without love? Was it possible for a woman not to love? Could a young, pretty woman, living in Paris, reading books, applauding actresses dying of passion on the stage, could such a woman go from adolescence to old age without her heart being touched one single time? He would never believe it of any other woman – why should he believe it of his mother?

Certainly she might have loved just like any other woman. For why should she be different from any other even though she was his mother?

She had been young, with all the poetic languishings that trouble the hearts of the young. Shut in prison in the shop beside the commonplace husband who always talked shop, she had dreamed of moonlight, travel, kisses in the shades of eventide. And then one day a man had come in, as lovers do in books, and he had talked like them.

She had loved the man. Why not? Because she was his mother! Very well then, why be blind and stupid to the point of refusing to accept the evidence because it was his mother?

Had she given herself to him? Of course she had, as this man had no other woman in his life. Yes of course, since he had remained faithful to the woman even when she was old and far

away; yes of course, since he had left all his fortune to his son –
their son!

Pierre jumped up, quivering with such a rage that he would
have liked to kill somebody. Arms outstretched and hand open,
he wanted to hit, bruise, crush, strangle! Who? Everybody,
his father, his brother, the dead man and his mother!

He began rushing home. What was he going to do?

As he was passing a tower near the signal-mast the strident
cry of the siren went off in his face. It was such a violent shock
that he nearly fell over, and staggered back into the granite
parapet. He sat down, his strength gone, broken by the din.

The first steamer to answer seemed quite close and appeared
at the harbour entrance as the tide was high.

Pierre turned round and saw its red eye, blurred by the fog.
Then in the misty glow of the electric lamps of the harbour a
great black shadow came into being between the two harbour
arms. Behind him the voice of the watch, the hoarse voice of an
old retired captain, bellowed:

'Ship's name?'

And equally hoarse there came through the fog the voice of
the pilot standing on the bridge:

'*Santa-Lucia.*'

'Country?'

'Italy.'

'Port?'

'Naples.'

Before his bewildered eyes Pierre thought he saw the plume
of fire above Vesuvius, while at the foot of the volcano fireflies
hovered in the orange groves of Sorrento or Castellamare.
How many times had he dreamed of those familiar names, as
though he knew the very scenes? Ah, if he could have gone
away, away at once, never mind where, never come back,
never write, never let anyone know what had become of him!
But no, he had to go home, home to his father's house and sleep
in his own bed.

To hell with it, he wouldn't go home, he would wait for day-

99

light. The voices of the sirens appealed to him. He got up again and began to march up and down like an officer keeping watch on deck.

Another ship was coming in after the first, enormous and mysterious. It was an English ship back from the Indies.

He saw several more emerging one by one out of the impenetrable shadows. Then as the dampness of the fog was becoming unbearable Pierre set off towards the town again. He was so cold that he turned into a sailors' tavern for some grog, and when the hot, spiced brandy had burned his palate and throat he felt a new hope being born within him.

He had been mistaken, possibly? He knew his uncontrollable mind so well! He had been mistaken, perhaps? He had been collecting evidence just as, when you are determined to believe a person guilty, you build up a case against an innocent man and it is easy enough to condemn him. When he had had a night's sleep he would think quite differently. So he went home to bed, and by sheer will-power dropped off in the end.

Chapter 5

But his body found hardly more than an hour or two of oblivion as it tossed and turned in a troubled sleep. When he woke up in the darkness of his hot and stuffy room he felt, even before his mind began working again, that painful oppression or *malaise* of the soul left in us by some grief we have slept on. It seems as though the misfortune which merely grazed us the day before has worked its way during our sleep into our very flesh and is bruising and exhausting it like a fever. Suddenly his memory came back, and he sat up in bed.

Then he started over again, slowly, one by one, all the arguments that had tormented his soul on the jetty while the sirens wailed. The more he thought the less he doubted. He felt impelled by his own logic as though a throttling hand were dragging him towards the unbearable certainty.

He was thirsty and hot and his heart was pounding. He got up to open the window for a breath of air, and when he was standing he heard a little noise coming through the wall.

Jean was sleeping peacefully and lightly snoring. Yes, he was asleep! He had foreseen no danger, guessed nothing! A man who had known their mother had left him his entire fortune. He was taking the money, thinking it only right and natural.

He was asleep, rich and contented, unaware that his brother was gasping in suffering and distress. A feeling of anger rose within him against this unheeding, happy snorer.

Only the day before he would have knocked on his door, gone in and sat by his bed and told him while he was still dazed by the sudden awakening: 'Jean, you mustn't keep this legacy because by tomorrow it might cast suspicion and dishonour on our mother.'

But today already he couldn't speak, couldn't tell Jean that he didn't believe he was their father's son. Now he had to keep this shameful discovery buried inside him, hide from everybody the shame he had detected. And nobody must discover it, not even his brother – above all not his brother.

He was hardly concerned at all now with mere respect for public opinion. He would willingly have let everybody accuse his mother so long as he and he alone knew she was innocent. How could he bear to live near her day and night and believe as he looked at her that she had brought forth his brother after the embraces of a stranger?

Yet how calm and serene she was, how sure she seemed of herself! Was it possible that a woman like her, pure in soul and righteous in heart, could fall a victim to passion without anything showing later of her remorse or of the memories that troubled her conscience?

Ah, remorse! remorse! It must have tortured her long ago in the early days, then faded as everything does. She would certainly have wept for her misdeeds and then she had gradually forgotten. Have not all women, every one of them, this gift of prodigious forgetfulness which enables them scarcely to recognize after a few years the man to whom they have given their lips and their whole body to kiss? The kiss strikes like lightning, love passes over like a storm, then life clears again like the sky and goes back to where it was before. Does anyone remember a cloud?

Pierre could not stay in his bedroom. This house, his father's house, was crushing him. He felt the roof pressing down on his head and the walls squeezing him to death. As he was very thirsty he lit his candle to go down and get a glass of cold water from the filter in the kitchen.

He went down the two flights of stairs, then as he was coming up again with the full carafe he sat down in his nightshirt on a step of the stairs where there was a breath of air and drank long draughts straight from the bottle, like an athlete out of breath. When he stopped moving the silence of the house oppressed him, and then he caught the smallest sounds one by one. First there was the dining-room clock whose ticking seemed to get louder each second. Then he heard some snoring again, the snoring of an elderly man, short, painful and harsh, his father's no doubt, and he winced at the thought, as though it had only just occurred to him, that these two men, snoring in the same house, father and son, had no connection with each other! No link, not even the most tenuous, united them, yet they did not know it! They addressed each other affectionately, kissed, enjoyed or were touched by the same things as though the same blood flowed through their veins. Yet two people born at the two most distant ends of the earth could not be more foreign to each other than this father and son. They thought they loved each other because a lie had grown up between them. This paternal and filial love rested on a lie, a lie impossible to reveal and that nobody could ever know of but himself, the real son.

And yet, and yet, suppose he were wrong? How could he know? Oh, if some likeness, however slight, could exist between his father and Jean, one of those mysterious resemblances between an ancestor and his great-grandsons, showing that a whole race issues directly from the same embrace! Being a doctor, he would have needed so little to recognize this – the shape of the jaw, the curve of the nose, the width between the eyes, the character of the teeth or hair, or even less, a gesture, a habit, some characteristic, some transmitted taste, some sign typical enough for a practised eye.

He pondered but could recall nothing, no, nothing at all. But he had not looked or observed very closely, not having any reason for discovering these imperceptible signs.

He stood up to return to his room and began slowly climbing the stairs, still thinking. As he was passing his brother's door he stopped with his hand out to open it. An urgent desire possessed him to see Jean at once, have a long look at him, surprise him in his sleep, while the face was at rest and the features were relaxed and all the grimacings of daily life had disappeared. Then he would grasp the hidden secret of his face and if any appreciable resemblance existed it would not escape him.

But if Jean were to wake up, what would he say? How could he explain this visit?

He stood still, with his fingers grasping the door-knob, looking for a reason, a pretext.

Then he suddenly remembered that a week earlier he had lent his brother a bottle of laudanum to deaden a toothache. He might be having trouble himself tonight and be coming to get the drug back. So he went in, but furtively, like a thief.

Jean was lying open-mouthed, sleeping a deep, animal sleep. His fair hair and beard made a golden patch on the white linen. He didn't wake up but stopped snoring.

Pierre leaned over him and studied him with an eager eye. No, this young man bore no resemblance to Roland, and for the second time the memory of the little vanished portrait of Maréchal came into his mind. He had to find it! When he saw it he might lose his doubts.

His brother stirred, probably disturbed by his presence or by the light of the candle through his eyelids. So the doctor withdrew on tiptoe to the door, which he shut noiselessly behind him, then went back to his own room, but not to bed.

Daylight was slow in coming. The hours struck one after another on the dining-room clock in a deep, solemn tone as though the little piece of clockwork had swallowed a cathedral bell. The sound came up the empty staircase, through walls and doors, and died away inside the rooms on the unhearing ears of the sleepers. Pierre had once again begun walking up and down between his bed and the window. What was he going to do? He felt too upset to spend that day with the family. He still wanted to be alone, at any rate until the next day, to think it over, calm down and find strength for the daily round which he would have to take up again.

All right, he would go to Trouville and watch the milling crowd on the beach. It would take his mind off things, give his thoughts a change of air, give him time to prepare himself to face the horrible thing he had discovered.

As soon as daylight appeared he washed and dressed. The fog had lifted and it was fine, beautiful. As the Trouville boat did not leave until nine the doctor thought he ought to say good-bye to his mother before going.

He waited for the time she usually got up, then went down. His heart was banging so hard as he touched her door handle that he paused for breath. His hand on the knob was limp and trembling, almost incapable of the trifling effort of turning it to go in. He knocked. His mother's voice answered:

'Who is it?'

'Me, Pierre.'

'What do you want?'

'To say good-bye because I'm spending the day at Trouville with some friends.'

'I'm still in bed.'

'All right, I won't disturb you. I'll give you a kiss when I get back tonight.'

He hoped he could get away without seeing her, without printing on her cheek the false kiss that made him heave in advance.

But she answered:

'Just a moment. I'll open the door and you can wait till I'm back in bed again.'

He heard her bare feet on the floor, then the sound of the bolt being drawn back. Then she called:

'Come in.'

He did. She was sitting up in bed, while by her side Roland was obstinately sleeping on, facing the wall with a silk handkerchief tied round his head. Nothing ever woke him except a shaking hard enough to pull his arm out of its socket. On fishing days Papagris the sailor rang the bell at the agreed time and the servant girl came up and dragged her master out of this invincible sleep.

As he crossed towards her Pierre looked at his mother. He suddenly felt he had never seen her before.

She held up her face and he kissed both cheeks, then sat on a low chair.

'Did you decide on this trip last night?' she said.

'Yes, last night.'

'Will you be back for dinner?'

'I don't know yet. In any case don't wait for me.'

He studied her with curiosity and amazement. This woman was his mother! This face, all of it, seen from babyhood as soon as his eyes could make anything out, this smile, this well-known, familiar voice, suddenly appeared new and different from what they had been to him until then. He now realized that because he loved her he had never looked at her. Yet it was certainly her, and not one of the smallest details of her face was unknown to him, but he was perceiving these little details clearly for the first time. His anxious scrutiny as he examined this beloved face, revealed it as different, with a character he had never discovered.

He got up to go, then, suddenly giving in to the invincible desire to know that had been nagging at him since yesterday:

'By the way, I thought I remembered that in the old days in Paris there was a little portrait of Maréchal in our sitting-room.'

She hesitated for a second or two, or at least he thought she did, then said:

'Oh yes.'

'What's become of it?'

Once again she could have been quicker with her reply:

'That portrait . . . let me see . . . I don't quite know. Perhaps it's in my desk.'

'Would you mind finding it?'

'Yes, I'll look. Why do you want it?'

'Oh it's not for me. I thought it would be quite natural to give it to Jean and would give him pleasure.'

'Yes, you're right, that's a nice thought. I'll look it out as soon as I'm up.'

He went out.

It was a blue day, without a breath of air. The people in the street seemed gay, business people going about their affairs, clerks off to their offices, shopgirls off to their shops. Some of them were humming for joy in the sunlight.

Passengers were already going aboard the Trouville boat. Pierre sat on a wooden bench right in the stern.

He asked himself:

'Was she upset by my question about the portrait or only taken by surprise? Has she mislaid it or hidden it? Does she know where it is or doesn't she? If she hid it, why?'

And his mind, always on the same track from deduction to deduction, came to this conclusion:

The portrait of a friend – or lover – had stayed in the sitting-room, visible to all, until the day when the woman, the mother, had been the first to notice, before anyone else, that this picture resembled her son. No doubt she had been looking out for this likeness for a long time, then, discovering it and watching it getting more striking, she had realized that everyone might notice it some time and had removed the disturbing little painting one night and hidden it, not having the heart to destroy it.

And now Pierre remembered quite clearly that this miniature had vanished a long, long time before they left Paris. It had disappeared, he believed, when Jean's beard was beginning to grow and had suddenly made him like the fair young man smiling from the frame.

The movement of the boat as it started disturbed and dissipated his train of thought, so he stood up and looked at the sea.

The little boat came clear of the jetties, turned left and, puffing, blowing and shuddering, headed for the distant coast that could be descried in the morning mist. Here and there the red sail of a heavy fishing-smack, motionless on the calm sea, looked like a big rock jutting out of the water. The Seine flowing down from Rouen appeared to be a wide arm of the sea separating two neighbouring territories.

In less than an hour they reached Trouville, and as it was the hour for bathing Pierre went on to the beach.

From a distance it might have been a long garden full of brilliantly coloured flowers. All along the great yellow sand-bank, from the jetty to the Roches-Noires, sunshades of all colours, hats of all shapes, dresses of all shades grouped in front of the bathing huts, lined up along the water's edge or scattered here and there, really did look like enormous beds of flowers in a huge meadow. And the indistinct sounds of voices far and near strung out in the limpid air – shouts, squeals of children being dipped in the sea, high-pitched laughter of women – made a continuous faint sound which you breathed in with the almost imperceptible breeze.

Pierre walked through the crowd of people, more lost, more cut off from them, more isolated, more sunk in his torturing thoughts than if he had been thrown from the deck of a ship a hundred leagues out from the coast. He passed close to them, heard a few sentences without taking them in, saw, without looking at them, men talking to women and women smiling at men.

But suddenly he seemed to wake up and see them distinctly, and a hatred of them rose within him, for they seemed happy and carefree.

Now he went on, passing near groups and skirting round them, seized by fresh thoughts. All these multicoloured dresses, covering the sand like beds of flowers, these pretty materials, these gaudy sunshades, the studied grace of corseted figures, all these ingenious inventions of fashion, from dainty shoe to extravagant hat, the seductive art of gesture, voice and smile, in fact the coquetry displayed on this beach, suddenly were re-vealed to him as an immense flowering of female perversity. All these bedizened women were out to please, seduce and tempt somebody. They had made themselves beautiful for men, all men except the husband they now had no need to conquer. They had made themselves beautiful for today's lover and tomorrow's, the stranger they had met, noticed or perhaps waited for.

And these men, sitting close to them, eyes gazing into eyes, speaking with mouth close to mouth, were calling to them, desiring them, hunting them like some lithe and elusive game apparently so near and so easy. So this great sea-front was nothing but a market for love in which some sold themselves and others gave themselves, the first set a price on their favours, the second merely promised them. All these women thought only of one thing, offering and making desirable their flesh which was already given, sold or promised to other men. And he realized that all over the world it was the same.

His mother had done the same as the rest, that was all! As the rest? No, exceptions did exist and many, many of them. Of course the ones he saw round him, rich, empty-headed, looking for love, belonged to the elegant, fashionable set or even to the ranks of the expensive ones for sale, for the straightforward ones who inhabited the red-light houses were not to be found on sea-fronts frequented by the legion of leisured ones.

The tide was coming in and gradually pushing the front rows of bathers back towards the town. Groups of people could be seen suddenly jumping up, carrying their seats with them and retreating from the yellow wave coming up with its fringe of lacy foam. Bathing machines pulled by horses were also moving up the beach, and along the boardwalk of the promenade that runs from one end of the beach to he other there was now an unbroken, dense, slow procession of elegant people in two opposing currents, jostling and mingling. Fidgeted and exasperated by this pushing about, Pierre fled through the town and stopped for lunch at a humble eating-house almost in the open country.

When he had finished his coffee he stretched his legs on two chairs outside, and as he had had an almost sleepless night he dozed off in the shade of a lime tree.

After several hours of rest he shook himself and realized that it was time to go back and catch the boat. So he set off, aching all over with the stiffness that had come over him in his sleep. Now he wanted to get back home and find out whether his mother had found Maréchal's portrait. Would she mention it first, or would he have to ask again? It was clear that if she waited again to be asked, she had a secret reason for not showing this picture.

But having regained his own room he hesitated about going down to dinner. He felt too upset. His feeling of nausea had not yet had time to settle. But he made up his mind and appeared in the dining-room just as they were sitting down.

Their faces were beaming with joy.

'Well now,' Roland said, 'is your shopping really going well? But I don't want to see anything before it is all in place!'

His wife answered:

'Oh yes, it's going very well. Only you have to think it out carefully to avoid things that don't go together. We are very busy with the furniture.'

She had spent the whole day with Jean in shops looking at furnishing fabrics and furniture. She wanted rich-looking materials, something a bit showy to catch the eye. Jean, on the other hand, was for something quiet and distinguished. So now, with all the patterns and possibilities, they had been going over their arguments again and again. She maintained that the client, the litigant, should be impressed, should get an impression of richness as soon as he entered the waiting-room.

Jean, on the contrary, only wishing to attract elegant and wealthy clients, wanted to win over the discerning people by his simple, infallible taste.

The argument, which had been going on all day, started again with the soup.

Roland had no opinion himself. He kept on saying:

'I don't want to hear anything about it. I shall go and see it when it's finished.'

So Mme Roland appealed to her elder son's judgement.

'Well, Pierre, what do you think?'

He was so worked up that he felt like answering by swearing at her. However, he said sharply in a voice unsteady with irritation:

'Oh, I'm all for Jean's opinion. I only like simplicity, which is to taste what honesty is to character.'

His mother answered:

'Don't forget we're living in a commercial town where good taste doesn't grow on trees.'

Pierre answered:

'What's that got to do with it? Is that a reason for imitating idiots? Just because my compatriots are stupid or dishonest have I got to follow their example? A woman won't sleep with a man simply because her neighbours have lovers!'

Jean burst out laughing.

'You use arguments by comparison that seem to be taken out of a moralist's book of maxims.'

Pierre made no answer. His mother and brother went back to talking materials and chairs.

He studied them as he had studied his mother that morning before setting off for Trouville, like a stranger observing, and indeed he felt he had suddenly come into a family of strangers.

His father, in particular, astonished both his eyes and his mind. This heavy, flabby man, smug and contented, was his own father! No, no, Jean wasn't in the least like him.

His family! For the past two days an unknown, evil hand, the hand of a dead man, had clawed at all the links that held these four creatures together and broken them one by one. It was all over and broken up. He had no mother, for he could not love her any more, not being able to venerate her with that absolute, tender, religious respect that a son's heart must have; he had no brother, since this brother was the child of a stranger. All he had left was a father, this coarse man he didn't love, try as he might.

All of a sudden:

'I say, Mother, did you find that portrait?'

She opened her eyes in surprise.

'What portrait?'

'The one of Maréchal.'

'No . . . I mean yes . . . I haven't found it but I think I know where it is.'

'What's this?' inquired Roland.

Pierre explained to him:

'A little miniature of Maréchal that used to be in our sitting-room in Paris. I thought Jean might be glad to have it.'

'Yes, of course, of course,' exclaimed Roland, 'I remember it perfectly, in fact I even saw it at the end of last week. Your mother had taken it out of her desk while going through her papers. It was Thursday or Friday. Don't you remember, Louise? I was shaving when you took it out of a drawer and put it on a chair on one side of you with a lot of letters, half of which you burned. Now isn't it funny that you should have handled that picture only two or three days before Jean's inheriting? If I believed in omens I should say that that was one!'

Mme Roland calmly went on:

'Oh yes, I know where it is. I'll go and fetch it in a minute.'

So she had lied! She had lied that very morning when she said to her son who had asked her what had become of that miniature: 'I don't really know, perhaps I've got it in my desk.'

She had seen it, touched it, held it, looked at it a few days before, then hidden it again in the secret drawer with some letters – his letters.

Pierre looked at the mother who had told a lie. He looked at her with the exasperated anger of a son deceived, robbed of his sacred love, and also with the jealousy of a man at last discovering a shameful infidelity after long remaining blind. If he had been the husband of this woman he, her son, would have seized her by the wrists, shoulders or hair and flung her to the ground punched, bruised, crushed! And he could say nothing, do nothing, show nothing, reveal nothing. He was her son, so he had nothing to avenge, he wasn't the one who had been deceived.

But he was, he had been deceived in his love and respectful reverence. She owed it to him to be without reproach, as do all mothers to their children. If the rage that filled him was verging on hatred, it was because he felt she was even more criminally guilty towards him than towards his father.

The love between man and woman is a voluntary pact in which the one who falls short is only guilty of perfidy, but when a woman has become a mother her duty is greater because nature has entrusted the human species to her. If she fails then she is a coward, unworthy and infamous.

'All the same,' Roland suddenly remarked, stretching his legs out under the table as he did every evening to sip his glass of black currant brandy, 'you can do worse than live in idleness when you've got a comfortable little income. I hope that Jean will give us some extra grand dinners now. What the hell if I do get a tummy-ache sometimes, what does it matter?'

Turning to his wife:

'Go and find that picture, duckie, as you've finished your dinner. I'd like to see it again, too.'

She got up, took a candle and went out. After what seemed a long absence to Pierre, though it had lasted less than two minutes, Mme Roland came back smiling and holding by its ring an old-fashioned gilt frame.

'Here you are,' she said, 'I found it almost at once.'

The doctor was the first to hold out a hand. He took the portrait and looked at it from a distance, at arm's length. Then, conscious that his mother was watching him, he slowly looked up at his brother to compare. Almost carried away by the violence of his feelings he nearly said: 'Look! It's like Jean!' Even if he did not dare to utter those terrible words, he betrayed what was in his mind by the way he compared the living face with the painted one.

They certainly had things in common – same beard, same forehead – but nothing exact enough to warrant declaring: 'That's the father and that's the son.' It was rather a family likeness, a relationship of faces of the same stock. But what was even more decisive in Pierre's eyes than this similarity of faces was that his mother had got up, turned her back and was pretending, far too slowly, to put away the sugar and black currant syrup into a cupboard.

She had realized that he knew or at least suspected.

'Let me have a look at that,' said Roland.

Pierre held out the miniature and his father moved the candle over to see properly. Then he murmured in maudlin tones:

'Poor chap! To think he was like that when we first knew him. Lord, how quickly time passes! Ah well, he was a nice-looking fellow then, and so pleasant in manner, wasn't he, Louise?'

As his wife made no answer he went on:

'And what an equable nature! I never saw him in a bad temper. Well, well, it's all over now, and there's nothing left of him except what he's left Jean. Anyhow, you can take my word for it that he's proved himself a good friend and faithful to the end. Even in death he hasn't forgotten us!'

Jean in his turn put out his hand to take the portrait. He studied it for a few moments, then, regretfully:

'I don't recognize him at all. I only remember him with white hair.'

And he gave the miniature back to his mother. She glanced at it, quickly looked away, as if in fear, then said in her normal voice:

'It belongs to you, Jeannot, as you are his heir. We'll take it to your new home.'

As they went into the sitting-room she put it on the mantel-piece by the clock, in its old position.

Roland filled his pipe, Pierre and Jean lit cigarettes. Usually as they smoked one walked up and down the room and the other sat in an armchair and crossed his legs. Their father always straddled a chair and spat at long range into the fire.

Mme Roland would sit on a low seat by a little table with the lamp on it and do embroidery, knit or mark some linen.

This particular evening she was beginning a tapestry for Jean's bedroom. It was a difficult and complicated piece of work and the beginning needed her full attention. Yet now and again her eyes, instead of counting the stitches, looked up quickly and furtively at the little picture of the dead man propped up against the clock. And the doctor, crossing the small room in four or five strides, hands behind back and cigarette between lips, caught his mother's eye each time.

It was as though they were spying on each other, as though a war had broken out between them, and Pierre's heart was wrung by a painful, unbearable *malaise*. Tortured and yet at the same time satisfied, he said to himself: 'How she must be suffering at this moment if she knows I've seen through her!' Each time he turned back towards the fireplace he paused for a few seconds to contemplate the blond face of Maréchal in order to show clearly that he was possessed by a fixed idea. And this little portrait, smaller than an open hand, seemed to be a living person, malignant and frightening, who had suddenly come into their home and family.

Then the front door bell rang. Mme Roland, normally so placid, jumped and betrayed to her doctor son the nervous state she was in.

Then she said: 'It must be Mme Rosémilly.' And again her eyes looked anxiously up at the mantelpiece.

Pierre understood her terror and anguish, or thought he did. Women have piercing eyes, quick brains and suspicious minds. Should the new arrival see this unknown miniature she would probably at once discover the likeness between this face and Jean's. Then she would know and understand everything! He was afraid, suddenly horribly afraid that this shame would be made public, and as the door was opening he turned round and slipped the little picture underneath the clock without his father or brother having noticed.

As he met his mother's eyes yet again he thought they looked changed, worried, desperate.

'Good evening,' said Mme Rosémilly, 'I've come to have a cup of tea with you.'

While they were fussing round her and inquiring about her health, Pierre disappeared through the open door.

When they realized he had gone they were amazed. Jean was annoyed because he feared that the young widow would be offended, and he muttered:

'What an oaf!'

Mme Roland said:

'You mustn't be angry with him, he's a bit under the weather today, and besides he's rather tired after his trip to Trouville.'

'No matter,' Jean went on, 'that's no reason for going off like a savage.'

Mme Rosémilly tried to calm things down by affirming:

'Oh no, he's just slipped away. You always slip off like that in the best circles if you go early.'

'Oh well,' said Jean, 'in the best circles, maybe, but you don't treat your family like that, and for some time now my brother has never done anything else.'

Chapter 6

NOTHING much happened in the Roland household for a week or two. The father went fishing, Jean set up house helped by his mother, Pierre was very morose and now only appeared at mealtimes.

When one evening his father asked:

'Why the devil do you always wear a funeral face? And it's not just today I've noticed it.'

Pierre replied:

'It's because I am weighed down by the burden of life.'

The old boy could make nothing of that, and said dismally:

'It really is too much. Ever since we've had the good fortune to have this legacy everyone looks miserable. It's just as though we'd had an accident or were in mourning!'

'As a matter of fact, I am,' said Pierre.

'You? Who for?'

'Oh, somebody you've never met and I was too fond of.'

Roland imagined it was some girl, some lady of easy virtue he had been after, and he asked:

'A woman, no doubt?'

'Yes, a woman.'

'Dead?'

'No, worse, lost.'

'Oh!'

Although he was astonished by this unforeseen burst of confidence in front of his wife, and by the strange tone his son adopted, he did not insist further, for he considered that such things are no concern of third parties.

Mme Roland appeared not to have heard, indeed she looked ill and was very pale. More than once already her husband, surprised to see her sit down as though she were collapsing in her chair, and hear her gasping as though she could not get her breath, had said to her:

'Really, Louise, you look bad. I'm sure you're overtaxing yourself by seeing Jean installed. Rest a bit, why ever don't you? The fellow's in no hurry, as he's well off.'

She shook her head without answering.

On this day her pallor was so marked that Roland noticed it again.

'Look here,' he said, 'this won't do at all, my poor old dear. You must look after yourself.'

Then turning to his son:

'You can see your mother's not well. Have you examined her at all?'

Pierre answered:

'No, I hadn't noticed anything wrong with her.'

That made Roland lose his temper.

'But good God, it's staring you in the face! What's the good of being a doctor if you can't even see your mother is indisposed! Look at her, just look at her! Really, you could peg out and this doctor would never notice!'

Mme Roland had begun to gasp for breath and looked so white that her husband exclaimed:

'Look, she's going to faint.'

'No, no ... It's nothing ... it'll pass, it's nothing!'

Pierre went near and stared hard at her.

'Look here, what's the matter?' he said.

She hastened to repeat softly:

'Nothing, I assure you, nothing.'

Roland had gone off to get some vinegar; he came back and held the bottle out to his son:

'Here you are ... but why don't you do something for her? Have you felt her pulse, anyway?'

As Pierre leaned over to feel her pulse she snatched her hand away so quickly that it hit another chair.

'Come along,' he said coldly. 'Let's look after you, as you are ill.'

Then she held up her arm for him. Her skin was burning and her pulse throbbing wildly. He murmured:

'It really is rather serious. You must take something to calm you down. I'll give you a prescription.'

As he was writing it out, bent over the paper, a little noise behind him – hurried sighs, breathlessness, stifled gasps – made him suddenly look round.

She was crying with her face buried in her hands.

Roland, quite distracted, asked:

'Louise, Louise, what is the matter? What on earth is the matter?'

She made no answer, but seemed torn by some horrible, deep sorrow.

Her husband was by way of taking her hands away from her face. She resisted, repeating:

'No, no, no!'

He turned to his son.

'But what is the matter with her? I've never seen her like this.'

'Nothing,' said Pierre, 'just a little nerve-storm.'

He felt a sense of relief in his own heart when he saw how tortured she was, and this pain of hers alleviated his own resentment and cut down the debt of hatred he owed his mother. He contemplated her like a judge pleased with his work.

But then suddenly she jumped up and made for the door at a speed that could not have been foreseen or stopped, and rushed to her room and shut herself in.

Roland and his son remained face to face.

'Can you make head or tail out of that?'

'Yes, it's a simple little nervous trouble that often shows itself at Mother's age. She'll probably have a lot more attacks like this.'

She did indeed, almost every day, and Pierre seemed to provoke them with something he said, as though he knew the secret of her strange, mysterious malady. He watched out for intervals of repose on her face, and with a torturer's ingenuity could with a single word revive the pain that had momentarily slumbered.

And yet he himself suffered quite as much. He suffered terribly because he no longer loved and respected her, but tortured her. When he had thoroughly re-opened the bleeding wound he had made in the heart of this wife and mother, when he realized how wretched and desperate she was, he went off on his own into the town, so tortured by remorse and shattered by pity, so horrified at having crushed her in this way with the contempt of her own son, that he felt like throwing himself into the sea to make an end of it all.

Oh, how he would have liked to forgive her now! But he couldn't, for he was incapable of forgetting. If only he had been able to spare her suffering, but he couldn't do that either because he was continually suffering himself. He came home at mealtimes full of compassionate resolves, and then as soon as he saw her and saw how her eyes, formerly so direct and honest, now turned away, fearful and wild, he lashed out in spite of himself, unable to check the barbed shafts that came to his lips.

The vile secret that they alone knew spurred him on against her. It was a venom now coursing through his veins and making him want to bite like a mad dog.

There was nothing to hinder him from constantly tormenting her, for Jean now lived almost all the time at his new flat and only came home to eat and sleep each night with his family.

Jean often noticed his brother's bitterness and violent outbursts, and attributed them to jealousy. He promised himself to put him in his place and teach him a lesson one day, for family life was becoming unendurable because of these continual scenes. But as he was now living on his own he was less upset by this brutal behaviour, and his love of a quiet life persuaded him to be patient. Moreover good fortune had turned his head and his thoughts scarcely ventured beyond things directly concerning himself. He would come home with his mind full of fresh little problems, concerned about the cut of a jacket, the shape of a felt hat, the correct size of a visiting card. And he never stopped talking about all the details of his home, shelves in the bedroom cupboard for the linen, pegs in the hall, electric burglar alarms to prevent any illegal entry.

It had been decided to celebrate his official moving-in with a picnic party at Saint-Jouin, and they would all come back after dinner for a cup of tea in his home. Roland was for going by sea, but the distance and the uncertain time of arrival by this means in the event of a head wind made the others reject his idea, and a wagonette was hired for the day.

They set off at about ten so as to get there for lunch. The dusty main road stretched across the Norman countryside which, with its undulating plains and tree-enclosed farms, looks like an endless park. In the vehicle, pulled at a gentle trot by two heavy horses, the Roland family, Mme Rosémilly and Captain Beausire were silent because of the deafening noise of the wheels, and kept their eyes shut in the cloud of dust.

It was harvest time. Contrasted with the dark green clover and bright green beet, the yellow corn lit up the country with a pale golden light. It seemed to have imbibed the sunlight that had poured down upon it. Harvesting was beginning here and there, and in the fields where scything had begun the men could be seen swaying to and fro as they moved their great wing-shaped blades over the ground.

After two hours the wagonette turned down a lane to the left past a windmill still working, a melancholy grey ruin half rotten and doomed, last survivor of the old mills; then it entered a pretty courtyard and drew up in front of a delightful house, a celebrated hostelry in the district.

The hostess, whom everybody called La Belle Alphonsine, came to the door all smiles and held out her hands to the two ladies who were hesitating because of the long jump down.

Some strangers, Parisians from Étretat, were already having lunch under an awning at the edge of a meadow shaded by apple trees, and inside the house could be heard voices, laughter and the clatter of crockery.

They had to eat in a private room as all the public ones were full. Suddenly Roland spied some prawn nets against the wall.

'Aha!' he cried, 'do they catch prawns here?'

'Yes,' answered Beausire, 'in fact they get more here than anywhere along the coast.'

'By Jove! Suppose we went after lunch?'

It so happened that low tide was at three, and it was decided that they would all spend the afternoon on the rocks looking for prawns.

They ate sparingly to avoid the rush of blood to the head when you have your feet in the water. They also wanted to save themselves up for the dinner, which was ordered on a lavish scale and was to be ready for their return at six o'clock.

Roland was jumping up and down with impatience. He wanted to buy special equipment for this kind of fishing, very like the nets they use for catching butterflies in the fields.

These are called *lanets*. They are little net pouches attached to a wooden ring at the end of a long stick. Alphonsine, always wreathed in smiles, lent him some. Then she helped the two women to improvise a way of dressing so as not to wet their clothes. She gave them skirts, heavy woollen stockings and rope-soled slippers. The men took off their socks and bought slippers and sabots from the local shoe-shop.

They set out, nets over shoulders and baskets on backs. In this get-up Mme Rosémilly looked quite charming, with an unsuspected peasant hoydenishness.

The skirt lent by Alphonsine, saucily turned up and caught with a few stitches to allow her to run and jump fearlessly on the rocks, displayed her ankle and lower calf, the firm calf of a strong and agile little woman. Her dress was loose to allow plenty of freedom of movement, and for her head she had found a huge yellow straw gardening hat with an enormous brim, one side of which was turned up with a sprig of tamarisk, which gave her a dashing and military look.

Since he had come into the money, Jean had been asking himself every day whether he was going to marry her or not. Each time he saw her he felt resolved to make her his wife, but then as soon as he was alone he thought that by putting it off he would have time to think it over. She had less money now than he had, for she only had an income of some twelve thousand francs, but it was in real estate, farms and land in Le Havre near the docks, and that might be worth a great deal later on. So their fortunes were roughly equal, and certainly he found the young widow extremely attractive.

As he watched her walking in front of him that day he thought: 'Come on, I must make up my mind. I certainly shan't do any better.'

They went down a little coomb, descending from the village to the cliffs, and at the bottom of this coomb the cliff-edge was eighty metres above the sea. Framed by the green slopes coming down from right and left, the great triangle of water, silver-blue in the sun, appeared in the distance, and a sail, only just visible, looked like an insect far below. The luminous sky merged so completely into the water that you couldn't possibly see where one ended and the other began; and against this bright horizon the two women, who were walking in front of the three men, made a contrast in their tightly fitting dresses.

Jean's eyes sparkled as he watched Mme Rosémilly's slender ankle, dainty leg, supple waist and large provocative hat running on ahead of him. This flight awoke his desire and spurred him on to the final resolve that suddenly comes to hesitant and timid natures. The warm air in which the scent of the hills, gorse, clover and grasses mingled with the salty smell of the newly uncovered rocks, excited him still more with a mild intoxication, and he made up his mind a bit more with each step, each second, each glance he cast at the lithe figure of the young woman; he decided to hesitate no longer, but tell her he loved her and wanted to marry her. The fishing trip would help him by making it easier for them to be alone together, and moreover it would be a nice place, a pretty scene for talking of love, as they stood in a pool of limpid water watching the long whiskers of the shrimps darting away under the seaweed.

When they reached the bottom of the coomb, on the very edge of the precipice, they spotted a little path going down the face of the cliff, and beneath them, between the sea and the foot of the precipice, about half-way, an amazing jumble of huge rocks that had fallen and were piled one upon another into a sort of grassy, uneven expanse formed by ancient landslides running southwards as far as the eye could see. On this long shelf of brushwood and grass shaken up, so to speak, by volcanic action, the fallen rocks looked like the ruins of a great vanished city which formerly overlooked the ocean and was itself over-looked by the endless white wall of cliffs.

'Isn't that beautiful!' said Mme Rosémilly, stopping to have a look.

Jean caught up with her and with beating heart offered his hand to help her down the narrow steps hewn out of the rock.

They went on ahead while Beausire, standing at attention on his short legs, offered his arm to Mme Roland, who had a bad head for heights.

Roland and Pierre brought up the rear, and the doctor had to drag his father along, for he was so upset by giddiness that he could only slide from step to step on his behind.

The young people went down first, walking fast, and sud-denly they came upon a wooden seat, which offered a resting place half-way down, and saw a trickle of clear water springing from a crevice in the cliff. It began by spreading into a hollow about the size of a wash-basin which it had dug out for itself, then, falling in a cascade about two feet high, it ran across the path carpeted at that spot with cress, and disappeared into the briars and grass across the sort of raised shelf strewn with fallen rocks.

'Oh I'm so thirsty!' exclaimed Mme Rosémilly.

But how could she drink? She tried to catch the water in her cupped hands but it ran through her fingers. Jean had an idea, he put a stone on the path and she knelt on it so as to drink from the spring itself, for her mouth was now at the same level.

When she raised her head, covered with myriads of tiny droplets all over her skin, hair, eyelashes and dress, Jean leaned over and murmured:

'How pretty you are!'

She answered in the sort of tone you use to scold a child:

'Now, now, be quiet!'

Those were the first words of love they exchanged.

'Come along,' said Jean, very embarrassed, 'let's get going before they catch us up.'

In fact quite near them they could see the back of Captain Beausire, who was coming down backwards so as to steady Mme Roland with both hands; and further away higher up Roland was still sliding down by sitting on his backside and propelling himself at tortoise speed with his feet and elbows, while Pierre preceded him to keep an eye on his movements.

The path was now less steep and turned into a sort of downhill track winding round the huge chunks of rock which had fallen from the mountain ages ago. Mme Rosémilly and Jean began running and were soon down on the shingle. They crossed this to get to the rocks, which stretched out in a long, level surface covered with marine vegetation in which gleamed numberless pools. The low tide was far away beyond this plain of slimy seaweed, shiny green and black.

Jean rolled up his trousers to just below his knees and his sleeves to his elbows so as to have no fear of wetting his clothes, then cried 'Forward!' and leapt boldly into the first pool he came to.

The lady, more cautious although she meant to paddle in the water in a minute, walked gingerly round the little pool because she was slipping on the slimy weed.

'Can you see anything?' she asked.

'Yes, your face reflected in the water.'

'If that's all you can see you won't have much of a catch.'

He murmured tenderly:

'Oh, of all the catches that's the one I would like best.'

She laughed:

'All right, you try and you'll see how it slips through your net.'

'And yet . . . if you wanted . . .?'

'What I want is to see you catch some prawns . . . that's all for the time being!'

'You are unkind. Let's go further along, there's nothing here.'

He gave her his hand to help her walk on the slippery rocks. She leaned on him timidly, and he suddenly felt a surge of love sweep over him, a growing desire, a hunger for her as though the sickness stirring within him had waited for that day to burst forth.

They soon came to a deeper rift in the rocks in which long weeds, delicate, strangely coloured, floating on the moving water as it flowed towards the distant sea along an invisible fissure, swayed like rose-pink or green hair.

Mme Rosémilly cried out:

'Look, look, I can see one, a big, a very big one over there.'

He saw it too, and resolutely stepped down into the hole although he got soaked up to the waist.

But the creature, waving its long whiskers, steadily backed away as the net approached. Jean pushed it towards the sea-weed, making sure he would catch it. But when it found itself hemmed in, it darted up over the net, across the pool and was gone.

The young woman, watching the chase with great excitement, could not help shouting:

'Oh, clumsy!'

He was vexed, and without thinking he dredged his net in some deep water full of weeds. When he brought it up to the surface he saw three big transparent prawns in it that he had caught without noticing their invisible hiding-place.

He triumphantly presented them to Mme Rosémilly, who was afraid to touch them because of the sharp, serrated barb on their heads.

But she made up her mind and taking the tips of their long whiskers between two fingers she put them one after another into her basket, with a bit of seaweed to keep them alive. Then when she found a shallower pool she stepped carefully into it, because the cold shock to her feet took her breath away, and began hunting on her own. She was dexterous and artful, with the quickness of hand and hunter's instinct that are essential. With almost every go she brought up prawns suddenly caught out by the skilful slowness of her pursuit.

Jean was now incapable of finding anything, but was following her step by step, touching her, leaning over her, simulating deep despair at his own lack of skill and pretending to be anxious to learn.

'Oh show me,' he said, 'do show me how!'

Then as their faces were reflected side by side in the clear water, made into a perfect mirror by the black vegetation on the bottom, Jean smiled at the face next to his looking up at him from the depths, and now and again threw a kiss at it with his fingertips.

'Oh you are tiresome,' she said. 'My dear man, you mustn't ever do two things at once.'

He replied:

'I'm only doing one. I love you.'

She stood up and said quite seriously:

'Look, what's come over you in the last ten minutes? Have you gone out of your mind?'

'No, I haven't gone out of my mind. I love you, and at last I have the courage to say so.'

They were now both standing in the salt pool with the water up to their calves and wet hands holding their nets, and they looked right into each other's eyes.

She went on in a tone of mock annoyance:

'How ill-advised of you to talk about that just now! Couldn't you wait until another day and not spoil my fishing?'

'I'm sorry, but I couldn't keep quiet any longer. I have loved you for a long time. Today you have bewitched me and made me lose my head.'

Then she suddenly seemed to make up her mind to talk business and give up pleasure.

'Let's sit down on this rock,' she said, 'and we can talk calmly.'

They climbed on to a rather high boulder and when they were settled side by side with legs dangling and the sun shining full on them, she went on:

'My dear friend, you're no longer a child and I'm not a young girl. We both know perfectly well what we are talking about and are capable of weighing all the consequences of our acts. If you have decided today to declare your love, I naturally conclude that you want to marry me.'

He was not quite expecting this clear statement of the situation, and answered lamely:

'Oh yes.'

'Have you spoken about it to your father and mother?'

'No, I wanted to know whether you would have me.'

She held out her wet hand and, as he eagerly took it:

'I am willing,' she said. 'I believe you are good and true. But don't forget that I shouldn't want to displease your parents.'

'Oh, do you suppose that my mother hasn't seen something coming, and that she would love you as she does if she were against a marriage between us?'

'That's true, and yet I'm a little uneasy.'

They fell silent. But he, on the contrary, was astonished that she appeared to be scarcely uneasy at all, but so rational. He had expected flirtatious behaviour, refusals meaning yes, the whole coquettish comedy of love mingled with fishing and accompanied by the splashing of water. And here it was all over, he felt tied, married in twenty words. They had nothing else to say since they were in agreement, and now were each slightly embarrassed at what had happened so quickly between them, even a little perplexed, not daring to say anything, not daring to go on fishing, at a loss what to do.

They were rescued by the voice of Roland.

'This way, this way, you youngsters. Come and look at Beausire. That chap is emptying the sea!'

The captain was indeed having a marvellous catch. Soaked up to the middle, he went from pool to pool, recognizing at a glance the best places and, with a slow, sure movement of his net, burrowing into all the cavities hidden under the seaweed.

The big transparent prawns, sandy grey, wriggled in his hand when he took them with a deft movement to throw into his basket.

Mme Rosémilly was surprised and delighted, and stuck to him, imitating him as best she could, almost forgetting her promise and Jean tagging on behind in a dream, throwing herself heart and soul into this childish fun of gathering these creatures from under the floating weeds.

Roland suddenly cried:

'Look, Mme Roland has caught us up.'

At first she had stayed on the beach alone with Pierre, for neither was keen on scampering about on the rocks and dabbling in the pools. Yet they hesitated to stay together. She was afraid of him, and her son was afraid of her and of himself, afraid of his own cruelty which he could not control.

So they sat down side by side on the shingle.

In the warm sun tempered by the sea breeze, before the vast, soft horizon of blue water flecked with silver, both of them were thinking at the same time: 'How lovely it would have been here once!'

She did not dare speak to Pierre, knowing full well that he would give her a harsh reply, and he did not dare speak to his mother because he also knew that despite himself he would speak brutally.

With the end of his stick he poked about at the round pebbles, stirred them up and hit them. She, staring at nothing, had picked up three or four little pebbles and was dropping them from one hand into the other, slowly and mechanically. Then her wandering eyes caught sight of her son Jean and Mme Rosémilly fishing in the middle of the seaweed. She followed their movements attentively, realizing vaguely, with her maternal instinct, that they were not talking as they did every day. She saw them lean over together when they looked at themselves in the water, stand up and stay face to face when they were examining their feelings, then climb up and sit on the rocks to pledge themselves to each other.

Their silhouettes stood out sharply, seemed alone on the horizon, and in the wide space of sky, sea and cliffs they took on something grand and symbolic.

Pierre was watching them too, and he suddenly gave vent to a sharp little laugh.

Without looking at him Mme Roland said:

'What is it?'

Still sneering he said:

'I'm taking lessons, learning how a man prepares himself to be a cuckold!'

She stiffened with anger and disgust, shocked by the word he used and furious at what she thought she understood.

'Who do you mean by that?'

'Jean, of course! It makes you laugh to see them together.'

In a low voice, trembling with emotion she murmured:

'Oh, Pierre, you are cruel! That woman is absolutely straight. Your brother couldn't find anyone better.'

He laughed outright, with an artificial, staccato laugh:

'Ha, ha, ha! Absolutely straight! All women are absolutely straight and all husbands are cuckolds. Ha, ha, ha!'

She made no answer, but got up and hurried down the shingle slope and at the risk of falling into holes concealed under vegetation, of breaking her leg or her arm, she almost ran, through pools, unseeing, straight in front of her, towards her other son.

Seeing her coming, Jean called out:

'Well, Mother, so you've decided to risk it?'

Without a word she seized his arm as though to say: 'Save me, protect me!'

Seeing how upset she was, he asked in amazement:

'How pale you are! What's the matter?'

She managed to say:

'I nearly had a fall. I was scared on those rocks.'

Jean led her, supporting her and explaining the fishing so as to get her interested. But as she was hardly listening and he was bursting to confide in somebody, he led her further off and whispered:

'Guess what I've done?'

'But . . . but . . . I don't know!'

'Guess.'

'I . . . I really don't know.'

'Well, I've told Mme Rosémilly that I want to marry her.'

She said nothing, her head was in a whirl and her mind so distressed that she could hardly take anything in. She echoed:

'Marry her?'

'Yes. Have I done the right thing? She is charming, don't you think?'

'Yes . . . charming . . . you've done the right thing.'

'So you approve?'

'Yes . . . I approve.'

'What a funny way you say that. Anyone would think that . . . you aren't pleased.'

'Oh yes I am . . . I am . . . pleased.'

'Really and truly?'

'Really and truly.'

To prove it she took him in her arms and kissed him full on the mouth, with great motherly kisses.

When she had dried her eyes, for they were full of tears, she saw further along the beach a body lying flat on its stomach, like a corpse, with its head buried in the shingle. It was the other one, Pierre, lost in thought, desperate.

Then she took her little Jean further off, to the water's edge, and they talked for a long time about this marriage on which he had set his heart.

The incoming tide drove them up to rejoin the others, then they all climbed back up the hill. They woke Pierre who was pretending to be asleep, and the dinner was a long one, washed down with lots of wine.

Chapter 7

ON the way home in the wagonette all the men slept except Jean. Beausire and Roland collapsed every five minutes on to a neighbouring shoulder which shoved them off again. Then they sat up, stopped snoring, murmured 'Lovely day' and fell back almost at once on to the other side.

By the time they reached Le Havre their slumber was so profound that they had great difficulty in shaking it off, and Beausire even declined to go up to Jean's flat, where tea was ready for them. He had to be dumped on his own doorstep.

The young lawyer was going to spend the night in his own home for the first time, and he was full of a great and rather childlike joy that on that very evening he could show his fiancée the flat in which she would soon be living.

The maid had gone, Mme Roland having declared that she would boil the kettle and serve the tea herself, for she did not like letting domestics sit up late for fear of fire.

Nobody had been inside the flat yet except herself, her son and the workmen, so that the surprise might be all the greater when they saw how pretty it was.

In the hall Jean asked them to wait. He wanted to light some candles as well as the lamps, and he left Mme Rosémilly, his father and brother in the dark and then called out: 'Come in!' throwing wide the double doors.

The glassed-in gallery, lit by a lustre and some coloured lights concealed in palms, rubber plants and flowers, looked at first like a stage set. For a moment they were all stunned. Roland, marvelling at this luxury, murmured 'Golly!' and was seized with a desire to clap his hands as one does at a grand finale in the theatre.

Then they passed on to the first reception room, which was quite small, with an old gold material on the walls matching the upholstery. The big consultation room was very simple, in pale salmon pink, and looked very distinguished.

Jean sat in the desk chair in front of his book-laden desk, and said in a solemn tone, slightly overdone:

'Yes, Madame, the letter of the law is quite clear and, pending the consent I said would be forthcoming, allows me to state with absolute certainty that within three months the affair we have discussed will have a happy conclusion.'

He looked hard at Mme Rosémilly, who began to smile as she looked at Mme Roland; and Mme Roland took her hand and squeezed it.

Radiant, Jean capered about like a schoolboy and shouted:

'Doesn't my voice carry well! This room would be excellent for pleading a case in.'

He began to declaim:

'If humanity alone, if that sentiment of natural kindness we feel towards any suffering, were the motive for the acquittal that we seek from you, we should call upon your pity, gentlemen of the jury, and your hearts as fathers and men; but we have the law on our side, and it is solely the legal point that we are going to bring before you . . .'

Pierre looked round at this home which might have been his, and he found his brother's fooling tiresome and considered him really too silly and fatuous.

Mme Roland opened a door on the right.

'This is the bedroom,' she said.

She had put all a mother's love into beautifying this room. The hangings were of Rouen cretonne imitating old Normandy cloth. A Louis XV design – a shepherdess in a medallion framed by the joined beaks of two doves – gave the walls, curtains, bed and chairs such a delightful air of rustic dalliance.

'Oh, it's charming!' said Mme Rosémilly, becoming a little subdued as she entered the room.

'Do you like it?' asked Jean.

'Enormously!'

'If only you knew how glad I am to know that!'

They held each other's gaze for a moment, with great tenderness and confidence in their eyes.

Yet she was slightly embarrassed and felt a little awkward in this bedroom which was to be her nuptial chamber. She had noticed as she came in that the bed was very wide, a real double bed, chosen by Mme Roland who had no doubt foreseen and desired her son's early marriage; nevertheless this maternal foresight pleased her, for it seemed to be assuring her that she would be welcomed in the family.

Then when they were back in the big room Jean suddenly threw open the door on the left, and they saw the circular dining-room, with its three windows and decorated to look like a Japanese lantern, into which mother and son had put all the fanciful imagination they were capable of. This room, with its bamboo furniture, Chinese porcelain figures and vases, gold-spangled silks, transparent blinds with glass beads in them looking like drops of water, fans nailed to the walls to catch up the draperies, with screens, sabres, masks, cranes made of real feathers, and all its little knick-knacks of porcelain, wood, paper, ivory, mother-of-pearl and bronze, had the pretentious and mannered appearance which unskilled hands and un-taught eyes bestow upon objects demanding the utmost tact, taste and artistic training. It was, however, the room which was most admired. Only Pierre had some reservations, offered with a somewhat bitter irony which hurt his brother's feelings.

On the table fruit was piled in pyramids and pastries rose in monuments.

Nobody was particularly hungry; they tasted some fruit and nibbled rather than ate the pastries. After an hour Mme Rosémilly asked if she might go home.

It was decided that M. Roland would see her to her door and

set out at once with her, while Mme Roland, the maid being absent, would cast a mother's eye round the place and see that her son lacked nothing.

'Shall I come back for you?' asked Roland.

She hesitated, then answered:

'No, dear, you go to bed. Pierre will bring me back.'

As soon as they had gone she blew out the candles, put away the pastries, sugar and liqueurs in a cupboard and gave the key to Jean, then went into the bedroom, turned down the bed, looked to see if the carafe had been filled with fresh water and the window had been properly shut.

Pierre and Jean had stayed in the smaller room, the latter still stung by the criticism made of his taste, and the former more and more irritated at seeing his brother in this abode.

They both smoked in their chairs and said nothing. Then Pierre suddenly stood up.

'Good Lord,' he said, 'the widow looked quite fagged out this evening. Excursions aren't very good for her.'

Jean felt himself possessed by one of those sudden and furious rages that come over good-natured souls when they have been hurt to the quick.

His emotion was so violent that it took his breath away and he could only stammer:

'I forbid you ever to say "the widow" again when you refer to Mme Rosémilly.'

Pierre turned loftily in his direction:

'I believe you are giving me orders. Are you taking leave of your senses, by any chance?'

Jean had drawn himself up too.

'No, I'm not. But I've had enough of your attitude towards me.'

'Towards you? Do you belong to Mme Rosémilly, then?'

'You'd better know that Mme Rosémilly is going to be my wife.'

His brother laughed louder.

'Ha, ha! That's lovely! I see now why I mustn't call her

"the widow" any more. But you have chosen a funny way of announcing your marriage.'

'I forbid you to make jokes about it . . . you understand, I forbid it!'

Jean went up to him, pale, his voice trembling with exasperation at the irony directed at the woman he loved and had chosen.

But Pierre suddenly lost his temper too. All the pent-up, impotent rage, repressed rancour and revolt he had managed to master for some time, and his silent despair, went to his head and made it swim as though he had had a seizure.

'How dare you! How dare you! And I order you to shut up, do you understand, I order it!'

Taken aback by this outburst, and in that state of mental confusion caused by rage, Jean was silent for some seconds, casting about for the thing, phrase or word that could wound his brother to the heart.

He started speaking again, forcibly controlling himself so as to strike hard and speaking slowly so as to make his words more hurtful:

'I've known for a long time that you're jealous of me, since the day when you began talking about "the widow" because you realized it hurt me.'

Pierre laughed the harsh and scornful laugh so characteristic of him.

'Ha, ha! Jealous of you? My God! What, me? . . . me? . . . me? And what am I jealous of? What, for God's sake? Your face or your intelligence?'

But Jean realized quite well that he had touched the real wound in his soul.

'Yes, you're jealous of me and always have been since we were children, and you went mad when you saw that this woman preferred me and didn't want you!'

Pierre now stammered out in exasperation at this idea:

'Me . . . me jealous of you? Because of that silly creature, that bird-brained female, that goose?'

Seeing that his blows had hit the target, Jean pursued the subject:

'And what about the day you tried to row harder than me in the *Perle*? And all the things you say in front of her to show off? Gosh, you're bursting with jealousy! And when I came into this money you saw red and hated me, and you've shown it in every way you could, you've upset everybody and never an hour passes but you spit the venom that's choking you.'

Pierre clenched his fists in rage and with an irresistible desire to throw himself at his brother and take him by the throat.

'Oh, hold your tongue, and don't you say anything about that money!'

Jean shouted:

'Your jealousy's oozing out of every pore. You never say a word to Father, Mother or me without its bursting out. You pretend to despise me because you are jealous. You pick quarrels with everybody because you're jealous. And now I am rich you can't contain yourself any longer, you've become venomous, you torture our mother just as if it were her fault...'

Pierre had retreated to the fireplace, mouth open and eyes staring, possessed by the sort of insane rage that makes a man commit a murder.

He repeated more softly but in a gasp:

'Shut up! Hold your tongue!'

'No I won't. For a long time now I've been wanting to tell you exactly what I think. You have given me the chance, so look out. I love a woman. You know that and yet you jeer at her in front of me, you goad me beyond endurance, so look out! But I'll smash in your viper's fangs for you. I'll force you to respect me.'

'Respect you – you!'

'Yes, me!'

'Respect you . . . you who've dishonoured us with your greed!'

'What did you say? Say it again, go on, say that again!'

'I say that you don't accept one man's money when you're supposed to be the son of another.'

Jean stood stock still, not comprehending, unnerved by the insinuation he could see coming.

'What? Say that again.'

'I am saying what everybody is whispering, the rumour that everybody is spreading, namely that you're the son of the man who has left you his money. Well, then, a decent fellow doesn't accept the money that dishonours his mother.'

'Pierre, Pierre, Pierre, how can you think of such a thing? You ... is it you uttering such a foul thing?'

'Yes, yes, it's me. Can't you see it's been killing me with misery for the past month, that I spend sleepless nights and days when I hide away like a wild animal, that I no longer know what I am saying or doing or what's going to become of me because I'm so wretched, so crazy with shame and grief; for I guessed it first, and now I know.'

'Pierre, be quiet. Mother is in the next room. Just think, she might hear us, I'm sure she can hear us.'

But Pierre had to unburden himself, and he told everything – his suspicions, his reasoning, his struggles, his certainty, and the story of the portrait, which had disappeared yet again.

He talked in short, clipped sentences, almost disjointedly, like a man in a state of hallucination.

He now seemed to have forgotten all about Jean and his mother in the next room. He was talking as though nobody was listening, simply because he had to talk, because he had suffered too much, constricted and covered up his wound too much. The wound had festered like an abscess, and now the abscess had burst and splashed over everybody. He had started walking up and down again as he almost always did, eyes staring straight ahead, gesticulating in a frenzy of despair, with sobs in his voice and fits of self-loathing, talking as though he were confessing his own misery and that of his family, as though he were unloading his grief on to the invisible, deaf winds which bore his voice away.

Horrified and suddenly almost convinced by his brother's blind violence, Jean had backed against the door behind which, he guessed, their mother had heard them.

She could not leave that room; you had to pass through this one. She had not come back, therefore she had not dared to.

All of a sudden Pierre stamped his foot and shouted:

'What a swine I am to have said that!'

And he rushed down the stairs, bareheaded.

The noise of the street door being slammed roused Jean from the deep torpor into which he had relapsed. A few seconds had passed, seconds longer than hours, and his soul had frozen into the dull torpor of idiocy. He realized perfectly well that he must think pretty quickly and act, but he dallied, having ceased to want to understand, to know, to remember, out of fear, weakness and cowardice. He was one of those temporizers who always put things off until tomorrow, and when he had to make an immediate decision he still instinctively sought to gain a few minutes.

But the deep silence round him now after Pierre's ravings, the sudden silence of walls and furniture, together with the bright light from the six candles and two lamps, suddenly scared him so much that he felt like running away too.

So he lashed his thoughts and heart into action and tried to think things out.

He had never come up against any difficulty in his life. Some men let themselves be carried along like running water. He had been a diligent schoolboy so as not to be punished, and passed through his law examinations with regularity because he led an untroubled life. Everything in the world seemed quite natural and he hadn't bothered much about it. By temperament he liked orderliness, good behaviour and tranquillity, for there was nothing complicated in his nature, and in the face of this catastrophe he was like a man who has fallen into the water and has never learned to swim.

First he tried doubt. Had his brother lied out of hatred and jealousy?

And yet how could he have been so vile as to say such a thing about their mother if he had not been driven out of his mind by despair? And then Jean still sensed in his ears, his eyes, his nerves, and even in the depths of his flesh, certain of Pierre's words, certain cries of suffering, intonations and gestures so painful that they were overwhelming and as irrefutable as certainty itself.

He was still too crushed to move or find the will-power to do anything. His distress was becoming intolerable. Yet he felt that behind the door was his mother who had heard everything and was waiting.

What was she doing? Not a movement, not a shudder or a breath or a sigh betrayed the presence of a living soul behind that piece of wood. Had she run away? But where? If she had run away she must have jumped out of the window into the street!

A sudden panic possessed him, so quick and compelling that he smashed in rather than opened the door and fell into the room.

It looked empty. It was lit by a single candle on the chest of drawers.

Jean rushed to the window, which was shut and the shutters closed. He turned round, searching in the dark corners with alarm, and then saw that the bed curtains were drawn. He ran over and opened them. His mother was stretched out on the bed with her face buried in the pillow, which she had pulled over her head with her clenched hands so as to hear no more.

At first he thought she had suffocated herself. Then having taken her by the shoulders he turned her over, but she still clutched the pillow which hid her face and which she was biting to stop herself from screaming.

But the feel of this rigid body, with the muscles of its arms stiff with effort, revealed the shock of her unspeakable torture. The energy and strength with which she was holding this bag of feathers, with her fingers and teeth, over her mouth, her eyes and ears so that he could neither see her nor speak to her, gave him an idea, by the turmoil she threw him into, of the extent to which one can suffer. And his heart, his simple heart, was rent with compassion. He was no judge, not even a merciful judge, he was a man full of weakness and a son full of love. He remembered nothing of what the other man had told him, he neither reasoned nor argued, but just touched with both hands the inert body of his mother, and not being able to pull the pillow away from her face, he kissed her dress and called very loud:

'Mother, Mother! My own Mother, look at me!'

She might have been dead had not an almost inperceptible shudder, like the vibration of a taut rope, run through her whole body. He repeated:

'Mother, Mother, listen. It isn't true, I know quite well it isn't true.'

A spasm shook her body, she choked, then suddenly sobbed into the pillow. All her nerves relaxed, her stiff muscles went soft, her fingers came open and released the linen, and he uncovered her face.

She was pale and white, and drops of water were flowing from under her closed eyelids. He put his arm round her neck and kissed her eyes slowly, with long, sad kisses, wet with her tears, still saying:

'Mother, darling Mother, I know it isn't true. Don't cry, I know it isn't.'

She sat up, looked at him, and with one of those supreme efforts of courage such as it must cost in some cases to kill oneself, she said:

'No, it's true, my child.'

They remained speechless facing each other. For a few more moments she went on choking, thrusting her chest forward and her head back in order to breathe, then she mastered herself again and went on:

'It's true, my child. Why should I lie? It's true, and you wouldn't believe me if I lied.'

She looked demented. Terrified, he fell on his knees beside the bed and murmured:

'Don't say anything, Mother. Don't say anything!'

She got to her feet with frightening energy and determination.

'In any case I've nothing more to say, my child. Good-bye!'

She made for the door.

He caught her in his arms, exclaiming:

'What are you doing, Mother, where are you going?'

'I don't know, how can I know . . . There is nothing left for me to do . . . for I'm quite alone.'

She tried to struggle free. He held on to her, but could only find the one word to say: 'Mother . . . Mother . . . Mother.'

While still struggling to get away from this embrace she said:

'No, no, I'm no longer your mother now. I'm nothing at all to you or anybody else, nothing, nothing at all! You've neither father nor mother now, poor boy . . . good-bye!'

He realized at once that if he let her go now he would never see her again, and lifting her in his arms he carried her to an armchair and forcibly sat her down, then, kneeling in front of her and hemming her in with his arms:

'You're not leaving this house, Mother. I love you and I'm keeping you. I'm keeping you for good, you are mine!'

She murmured as though exhausted:

'No, my poor boy, it isn't possible now. You're crying tonight, but tomorrow you would throw me out. You wouldn't forgive me, either.'

He replied with an outburst of such genuine love: 'What, me! How little you know me!' that she cried out, took his head by the hair with both hands, pulled it violently towards her and kissed his face hysterically.

But then she remained still, with her cheek against her son's, feeling the warmth of his skin through his beard, and whispered into his ear:

'No, my little Jean. Tomorrow you wouldn't forgive me. You think you would, but you are deceiving yourself. You have forgiven me this evening, and your forgiveness has saved my life, but you mustn't see me ever again.'

Holding her close, he repeated:

'Mother, don't say that!'

'Yes, my dearest, I must go away. I don't know where, nor how I am to set about it, nor how I shall explain, but go I must. I would never dare to look at you nor kiss you, don't you see?'

Then it was his turn to whisper in her ear:

'Mummy, you will stay because I want you to, because I need you. And you are going to swear to obey me, now!'

'No, my child!'

'Oh Mother, you must, you understand, you must!'

'No, my child, it's impossible. It would mean condemning us all to hell. I have known for a month now what that torment means. You are feeling emotional, but when that has passed and you look at me as Pierre does, when you remember what I have told you! Oh my dear little Jean, just think . . . think that I am your mother!'

'I won't let you leave me, Mother. I've only got you!'

'But just think, my son, from now on we shan't be able to see each other without blushing, without my feeling that I'm dying with shame, and without your eyes forcing mine to look away.'

'That's not true, Mother.'

'Yes, yes, yes it is! Oh, from the very first day I have understood perfectly well all your poor brother's struggles. Now, when I think I can hear his footsteps in the house, my heart thumps fit to burst my chest. When I hear his voice I feel I'm going to faint. But then I still had you! Now I've lost you as well. Oh Jean, do you believe I could live between the two of you?'

'Yes, Mother. I shall love you so much that you'll stop thinking about it.'

'Oh, just as though that were possible!'

'Yes, it is possible.'

'How do you expect me to stop thinking about it between your brother and you? Won't you think about it yourself?'

'I swear I shan't!'

'But you will, every moment of the day.'

'No, I swear not. And listen: if you go away I shall join up and get myself killed.'

This childish threat quite overcame her, and she embraced Jean and caressed him with passionate tenderness. He went on:

'I love you more than you think, much more, much more. Look here, do be sensible. Try to stay for just one week. Will you promise me a week? You can't refuse that?'

She put her hands on Jean's shoulders and held him at arm's length.

'My child, let's try to be calm and not emotional about it. Let me talk to you first. If once I were to hear on your lips what I have been hearing your brother saying for a month, if once I were to see in your eyes what I read in his, if I were to guess just from a word or a look that I am as odious to you as I am to him . . . within an hour, do you hear, within an hour, I should be gone for ever!'

'Mother, I swear . . .'

'Let me speak. For the past month I have gone through everything a poor creature can suffer. From the moment I realized that your brother, my other son, suspected me and was piecing together the truth minute by minute, every moment of my life has been a torture impossible to describe.'

Her voice was so grief-stricken that her torture, like a contagion, made Jean's eyes fill with tears.

He tried to kiss her, but she pushed him away.

'Leave me alone, and listen . . . I've a lot to tell you before you can understand . . . but you won't understand . . . that is to say . . . if I were to stay . . . I should have to . . . No, I can't!'

'Go on, Mother, tell me.'

'All right, I will. At least I shan't have deceived you . . . You want me to stay with you, don't you? For that to happen, for us to be able to go on seeing each other, talking and meeting all day long at home, for now I daren't open a door for fear of finding your brother behind it, for all that to happen not only must you forgive me – and nothing hurts so much as forgiveness

– but you mustn't harbour any resentment for what I have done . . . You must feel yourself strong enough, and sufficiently different from everybody else, to be able to tell yourself that you aren't Roland's son without blushing for it and despising me! I've suffered enough. I've suffered too much, I can't stand any more, I can't stand any more. And it doesn't date from yesterday, but from long ago . . . But you'll never understand that. For us to be able to live together and embrace each other, my little Jean, get it clear in your mind that even if I was your father's mistress I was his wife still more, his real wife, that I feel no shame in the depths of my heart and have no regrets, that I still love him, dead though he is, and shall always love him, that I have never loved anyone else but him, that he has been all my life, all my joy, all my hope and consolation, everything to me, everything, for so long! Listen, my dear boy, as God is my witness, I should never have had anything worth while in my existence if I hadn't met him – nothing ever, not the slightest tenderness or sweetness, not one of those hours that make us so sorry to be growing old, nothing! I owe him everything! I have had nobody but him in the world, and then you two, your brother and you. Without you it would be empty, black and void as the night. I should never have loved anything, known anything, desired anything. I shouldn't even have wept, for I have wept, Jean. Oh yes, I've wept since we came down here. I had given myself to him, body and soul, for ever, joyfully, and for more than ten years I was his wife as he was my husband in the eyes of God, who had created us for each other. And then I realized that his love was waning. He was always kind and considerate, but I no longer meant the same to him as I had done. It was over. Oh, how I wept! How miserable and deceptive life is! Nothing lasts . . . And then we came here and I never saw him again, he never came. He promised to in all his letters. I was always waiting for him . . . I never saw him again . . . and now he is dead. But he still loved us because he has thought of you. I shall love him to my last breath and never disown him, and I love you because you are his child and I could never be ashamed of him in front of you! Never, you understand? If you want me to stay you must accept the fact of being his son and we must talk about him sometimes, and you must love him a bit and we must think of him when we look at each other. If you don't want to do that, or you can't, then good-bye, my child, it is impossible for us to stay together now. I shall do what you decide.'

Jean answered very gently:

'Stay, Mother!'

She clasped him in her arms and began crying again, then, with her cheek close to his, she went on:

'Yes, but what about Pierre? What are we going to do about him?'

Jean murmured:

'We'll find some way. You can't live with him.'

The mere thought of her elder son made her wince with anguish.

'No, I can't face that any more, no, no!'

Throwing herself on Jean's breast she cried out in distress:

'Save me from him, won't you, my dear boy, save me, do something, anything ... find a way, save me!'

'Yes, Mother, I'll try.'

'No, at once ... you must ... At once, don't leave me! I'm so frightened of him, so afraid!'

'Yes, I'll think of something. I promise.'

'Oh, quick, quick! You can't imagine what I feel when I see him.'

Then she murmured very softly into his ear:

'Keep me here, in your home.'

He hesitated, thought it over, and with his practical common sense saw at once the danger of such an arrangement.

But he had to go through a great deal of reasoning and discussion in order to combat her hysterical terror with sensible arguments.

'Just for tonight,' she said, 'just tonight. Tomorrow you can give Roland to understand that I didn't feel well.'

'It isn't possible because Pierre will have got home by now.

Come along, be brave. I promise you I'll work it all out to-morrow. I'll be there by nine. Come along, put your hat on and I'll take you home.'

'I'll do as you wish,' she said with a childlike surrender, timid and grateful.

She tried to stand up, but the shock had been too great and she could not yet stand.

He made her drink some water with sugar in it, sniff some smelling-salts and rubbed her temples with vinegar. She let him do anything with her, exhausted and relieved like a woman after childbirth.

Eventually she was able to walk and took his arm. It was three in the morning by the time they passed the Town Hall.

At the street door he kissed her and said: 'Good-bye, Mother, be brave.'

She furtively went up the silent staircase and into her bed-room, undressed quickly, and as she slipped into bed beside the snoring Roland she felt once again the old excitement of those bygone adulteries.

Pierre was the only one in the house still awake, and he heard her come home.

Chapter 8

BACK in his own flat, Jean sank on to a sofa, for the sorrows and worries that made his brother want to run away like a hunted beast, acting differently on his lethargic nature, took all the strength out of his arms and legs. He felt so limp that he could not make a single movement or get as far as his bed, limp in body and mind, crushed and desolate. He was not wounded, as Pierre had been, in the purity of his filial love, in the secret dignity which is the protection of proud hearts, but shattered by a blow of fate that at the same time threatened his own most treasured schemes.

When his soul had at last calmed down, and his thoughts had cleared like a pool after it has been churned up, he looked at the situation that had been revealed to him. If he had learned the secret of his birth in any other way he would certainly have been outraged and felt a deep resentment, but after his quarrel with his brother, after this violent and brutal accusation which had shaken his nerves, the heartbreaking emotion of his mother's confession took away all his energy to revolt. The shock to his feelings had been violent enough to sweep away all the prejudices and pious susceptibilities of natural morality on an irresistible wave of emotion. Not that he was the fighting type. He disliked fighting anybody, and least of all himself, so he resigned himself and with his instinctive penchant and innate love of quiet and a pleasant and peaceful life, he immediately took fright at the upsets that were going to develop round him and consequently affect him. He had a feeling that they were unavoidable, and to thrust them out of the way he resolved to make superhuman efforts to be energetic and active. Therefore at once, from tomorrow, the matter must be settled, for he also had from time to time that imperious need for instant solutions which is the only strength of weak people, incapable of a sustained effort of will. Moreover his lawyer's mind, trained to untangle and examine complicated situations and matters of an intimate nature in families at loggerheads, at once saw all the immediate consequences of his brother's state of mind. In spite of himself he envisaged these consequences from an almost professional standpoint, as though he were settling the future relationships between clients after a moral upheaval. For him continual contact with Pierre was becoming decidedly out of the question. He could easily avoid him by staying in his own place, but it was also unthinkable that their mother should go on living under the same roof as her elder son.

For a long time he lay still on the cushions meditating, devising and rejecting solutions, but he could find nothing satisfactory.

Then an idea struck him: would a decent man keep this money he had received?

At first he answered 'No,' and decided to give it to the poor. It was hard, but still ... He would sell his furniture and work like anybody else, as everybody has to do at the start. With this manly and painful resolution to spur on his courage he got up and went and put his forehead against the window-pane. He had been poor, and poor he would become again. It wouldn't kill him, after all. He stared at the gas-lamp opposite him across the street. A woman, obviously out very late, walking along the pavement, suddenly reminded him of Mme Rosémilly, and he was stabbed to the heart by the profound emotion into which we can be plunged by some torturing thought. All the heartbreaking consequences of his decision were clear to him at the same time. He would have to give up marrying this woman, give up happiness, give up everything. Could he act in this way now that he had pledged himself to her? She had accepted him as a rich man. Even poor, she would still accept him, but had he the right to ask her and impose this sacrifice upon her? Would it not be better to keep this money as if it were in trust to be paid back later to the poor?

Within his soul, in which egotism assumed a mask of virtue, all the disguised forms of self-interest struggled and fought. The first scruples gave way to ingenious arguments, then reappeared, then disappeared again.

He went and sat down again, seeking for some deciding motive or all-powerful pretext to put an end to his hesitations and convince his natural uprightness. A score of times already he had asked himself this question: 'As I am this man's son, and know it and accept the fact, isn't it natural that I should also accept his legacy?' But this argument could not silence the 'No' whispered by his inmost conscience.

Suddenly he thought: 'As I am not the son of the man I thought was my father I can't accept anything else from him either during his lifetime or after his death. It would be neither decent nor just. It would mean robbing my brother.'

This new way of looking at it having given him some relief and appeased his conscience, he went back to the window.

'Yes,' he told himself, 'I must give up my share of the family inheritance and cede it all to Pierre, as I am not his father's child. That's only fair. Well, then, isn't it also fair that I should keep my own father's money?'

Having acknowledged that he could not benefit from Roland's money and decided to give it up altogether, he consented to keep Maréchal's money and resigned himself to it, for if he refused to touch either he would reduce himself to sheer beggary.

Once this delicate question was settled he returned to the matter of Pierre's presence in the family. How could he be got out of the way? He was giving up hope of discovering any practical solution when the siren of a liner entering the harbour seemed to bring an answer by suggesting an idea.

Then he stretched out on his bed fully dressed and dreamed until dawn.

At about nine he went out to test whether it was possible to carry out his idea. After some inquiries and calls he went to his parents' home. His mother was waiting for him, shut up in her room.

'If you hadn't come I wouldn't ever have dared to go down-stairs.'

At once Roland could be heard bellowing up the stairs:

'Aren't we having any food today, for God's sake?'

Nobody answered, so he bawled:

'Joséphine, for God's sake what are you up to?'

The voice of the girl came up from the bowels of the earth:

'All right, M'sieu, what do you want?'

'Where is the mistress?'

'Madame's upstairs with Monsieur Jean!'

Then he shouted up to the floor above:

'Louise!'

She opened the door and called down:

'What is it, dear?'

'Aren't we having any food today, for the Lord's sake?'

'All right, dear, we're coming down.'

She came down, and Jean after her.

Seeing him Roland exclaimed:

'Well, you here too? Getting sick of your home already?'

'No, Father, but I wanted to talk to Mother this morning.'

Jean went up to him with outstretched hand, and when he felt the old man's paternal handshake squeezing his fingers he was gripped by a strange and unforeseen emotion, the emotion of separations and farewells with no hope of return.

Mme Roland asked:

'Pierre isn't here yet?'

Her husband shrugged.

'No, but never mind, he's always late. Let's start without him.'

She turned to Jean.

'You ought to go and fetch him, dear. He gets so upset when we don't wait for him.'

'Yes, Mother, I'll go.'

He went off. He ran upstairs with the nervous determination of a timid man facing a fight.

When he knocked on the door Pierre answered:

'Come in.'

He did so.

His brother was bent over his table, writing.

'Good morning,' said Jean.

Pierre stood up.

'Good morning.'

They shook hands as though nothing had happened.

'Aren't you coming down to breakfast?'

'Well...that is...I've got a lot of work to do.'

The elder son's voice faltered and his anxious eyes asked the younger what he was going to do.

'They're waiting for you.'

'Oh...is er...is our mother down?'

'Yes, in fact she sent me up to find you.'

'Oh, in that case I'll come down.'

Outside the dining-room door he hesitated to be the first to appear, but then he opened it with a jerk and saw his father and mother sitting at the table facing each other.

He went to her first, without raising his eyes or saying a word, he leaned over for her to kiss his forehead, as he had been doing for some time instead of kissing her on both cheeks as of old. He sensed that she brought her lips near, but didn't feel them touch his skin, then he straightened up with beating heart after this pretence at a caress.

He was wondering: 'What did they say to each other after I left?'

Jean affectionately kept on saying 'Mother' and 'dear Mummy', looking after her, serving her and pouring out a drink for her. Then Pierre realized that they had shared their grief together, but he couldn't make out what they were thinking. Did Jean think that his mother was guilty or that his brother was a blackguard?

And all the reproaches he had heaped upon himself for having uttered the horrible thing assailed him once again, tightening his throat and shutting his mouth, preventing him from eating or talking.

Now he was possessed by an intolerable urge to rush away, get out of this house which was no longer home, away from these people whose links with him were scarcely perceptible. He would have liked to get away there and then, anywhere, feeling that it was all over and he couldn't stay near them, that he would always be torturing them in spite of himself, if only by his presence, and that they would make him suffer endless, unbearable torments.

Jean was talking, discussing something with Roland. Pierre was not listening, never even heard. But all the same he thought he caught some intention in his brother's voice, and paid heed to the meaning of the words.

Jean was saying:

'It seems that she will be the finest vessel in their fleet. They talk of 6,500 tons. She will make her maiden voyage next month.'

Roland was astonished:

'What, already? I thought she wouldn't be ready to put to sea this summer.'

'Oh yes she will, they have pushed on with the job like mad so that the first crossing can come off before the autumn. This morning I went into the offices of the Company and talked to one of the directors.'

'Oh, which one?'

'M. Marchand, the close friend of the Chairman of the Board.'

'Really! Do you know him?'

'Yes, and besides, I had a little favour to ask him.'

'Oh, then you can arrange for me to go over every part of the *Lorraine* when she comes into harbour, can you?'

'Certainly, it's quite simple.'

Jean appeared to be hesitating, looking for the right words, trying to lead up to some elusive transition. Then he went on:

'In fact the life they lead on these big transatlantic liners is very agreeable. They spend more than half the time ashore in two wonderful cities, New York and Le Havre, and the rest at sea with delightful people. You can even strike up very pleasant friendships with the passengers, and very useful ones for later on, yes, very useful. Just consider that the captain can make, with savings on coal, as much as 25,000 fr. a year, if not more...'

Roland uttered a 'Golly!' followed by a whistle, which signified a profound respect for the sum and for the captain.

Jean went on:

'The purser can reach 10,000 and the doctor has 5,000 fixed salary, with lodging, board, light, heat, service etc. thrown in. Which is the equivalent of 10,000 at least. It's very good.'

Pierre had looked up, he caught his brother's eye and understood.

After a little hesitation he asked:

'Are they difficult to get, jobs as ship's doctor on a trans-atlantic liner?'

'Yes and no. It all depends on circumstances and who's backing you.'

There was a long pause and then the doctor went on:

'It's next month that the *Lorraine* sails?'

'Yes, on the 7th.'

They fell silent.

Pierre was thinking. It certainly would be a way out if he could sign on as a ship's doctor on this liner. Later on he could see – he might leave, perhaps. Meanwhile he could earn his living without asking anything of his family. Two days earlier he had had to sell his watch because now he couldn't hold out his hand for money from his mother! But apart from that he had no resources, no way of eating any other bread than the bread of his inhospitable home, of sleeping in any other bed under any other roof. Then he ventured hesitantly:

'I would gladly sail in her if I could.'

Jean asked:

'Why couldn't you?'

'Because I don't know anybody in the Transatlantic Company.'

Roland was appalled.

'And what about all your fine plans for success?'

Pierre murmured:

'There are times when you have to be prepared to sacrifice everything and give up your cherished hopes. In any case this is only a start, a means of saving a few thousand francs so as to set myself up later.'

His father was at once convinced.

'Yes, that's true. In two years you could set aside six or seven thousand francs which will see you a long way if properly managed. What do you think, Louise?'

She answered in a soft, almost inaudible voice:

'I think Pierre is right.'

Roland shouted:

'Then I'll go and have a word with M. Poulin whom I know quite well. He is a judge in the Commercial Court and concerned with the Company's affairs. There is M. Lenient, too, the shipowner, who is very much in with one of the vice-chairmen.'

'Would you like me to sound M. Marchand today?' Jean asked his brother.

'Yes, I'd like you to.'

After a few moments' thought Pierre went on:

'And yet the best way might be to write to my professors at the Medical School, who thought very well of me. Often they ship away duds on those boats. Enthusiastic letters from professors like Mas-Roussel, Rémusot, Flache and Borriquel would settle the matter in an hour much better than all the fishy recommendations. It would be enough to get your friend M. Marchand to lay those letters before the Board.'

Jean agreed absolutely.

'Your idea is excellent, excellent!'

He was smiling, quite reassured, almost happy and sure of

success, being incapable of keeping up miseries for long.

'You must write off today,' he said.

'In a minute, in fact at once. I'll go now. I won't have any coffee this morning, I'm too worked up.'

He got up and went out.

Jean turned to his mother.

'What are you going to do now, Mother?'

'Nothing. I don't know.'

'Will you come with me to Mme Rosémilly's?'

'Er . . . yes . . . yes.'

'You know . . . I simply must go there today.'

'Yes, yes, that's true.'

'Why must you?' asked Roland who, to be sure, made a point of never understanding what was said in his hearing.

'Because I promised her I would.'

'Oh well, that's different, of course!'

He began filling his pipe, whilst mother and son went up-stairs to get their hats.

When they were in the street Jean asked her:

'Would you like my arm, Mother?'

He never normally offered it, for they used to walk side by side. She accepted and leaned on him.

For some time they did not speak, then he said:

'You see Pierre is perfectly willing to go away.'

'Poor boy!' she murmured.

'Why poor boy? He won't be at all unhappy on the *Lorraine*.'

'No . . . I know that, but I'm thinking of so many things.'

She went on musing for some time, looking at the ground, keeping step with her son, then in that strange voice people sometimes use for bringing out a thought they have long been turning over in secret:

'How ugly life is! If for once you find a little sweetness in it you are wicked to enjoy it and pay very heavily for it later.'

He said very gently:

'Don't talk about that any more, Mother!'

157

'How is that possible? I think about it all the time.'

'You'll forget.'

She fell silent again and then, with profound regret:

'How happy I might have been had I married another man!'

Now she was working herself up against Roland, throwing all the responsibility for her misconduct and her unhappiness upon his ugliness, his stupidity, his clumsiness, the stodginess of his mind and his commonplace appearance. It was because of that, the vulgarity of this man, that she had deceived him, reduced one of her sons to desperation and made to the other the most painful confession that can wound a mother's heart.

She murmured: 'It's so awful for a young girl to marry a husband like mine!' Jean made no answer. He was thinking of the man whose son he had thought he was until now, and perhaps the confused notion he had long had of his father's mediocrity, the constant bitterness of his brother, the scornful indifference of other people and even the contempt of the servant girl for Roland, had all prepared his soul for the terrible admission of his mother. All this made it less painful to him to be the son of another, and if, after the great emotional shock of the previous day, he had not suffered the reaction of disgust, indignation and anger Mme Roland had dreaded, it was because for quite a long time he had been subconsciously resenting being the offspring of this amiable oaf.

They had reached Mme Rosémilly's house.

She lived on the Sainte-Adresse road, on the second floor of a large building which she owned. From her windows there was a view over the whole roadstead of Le Havre.

When she saw Mme Roland coming in first, instead of holding out her hands as usual she opened her arms and embraced her, for she guessed the object of her coming.

The furniture in the drawing-room, in embossed velvet, was always under loose covers. On the walls, papered in a flower pattern, were four engravings bought by her first husband, the captain. They depicted sentimental sea-scenes. In the first could be seen a fisherman's wife waving a handkerchief on the shore while the sail of the boat carrying her man away was disappearing over the horizon. In the second the same woman, on her knees on the same shore, was wringing her hands while watching from afar, beneath a sky full of lightning, on a sea with improbable waves, her husband's bark about to founder.

The two other pictures showed similar scenes in a higher class of society.

A blonde young woman leans pensively over the rail of a great liner, leaving home. She looks at the already distant coast with eyes moist with tears and regrets.

Whom has she left behind her?

Then, the same young woman, seated near a window overlooking the ocean, has fainted in her chair. A letter has fallen from her lap to the floor.

He is dead! How terrible!

Visitors were usually much affected and taken with the banal pathos of these obvious and poetic subjects. They understood at once, with no explanation or head-scratching, and pitied the poor women though they didn't know the exact nature of the distress of the more distinguished of the two. But this very doubt encouraged reverie. She must have lost her betrothed! On entering the room one's eye was caught by these four pictures, and held by a sort of fascination. It left them only to return and go on contemplating for ever the four expressions of the two women, who were as alike as two peas. Above all there emanated from the clear-cut drawing, beautifully finished and sharply defined, elegant as a fashion plate, as well as from the gleaming frames, a sensation of what is right and proper, enhanced by the rest of the furniture.

The chairs were always arranged in precisely the same order, some against the wall, others round the coffee-table. The immaculate white curtains hung in such straight and regular folds that you felt like disarranging them a bit, and never a speck of dust dimmed the glass dome under which the Empire clock, a globe borne by a kneeling Atlas, seemed to be like a melon ripening indoors.

As they sat down, the two women slightly changed the normal position of the chairs.

'You haven't been out today?' inquired Mme Roland.

'No, I admit I'm a bit tired.'

And she recalled, by way of thanks to Jean and his mother, all the pleasure she had had from the outing and the fishing.

'You know,' she said, 'I ate my prawns this morning. They were delicious. If you are willing we'll go again one of these days!'

The young man cut in:

'Before going on another one, suppose we complete the first?'

'What do you mean? But surely it is finished.'

'Oh, Madame, I caught something among those rocks at Saint-Jouin that I also want to take home!'

She went all innocent and arch:

'Did you? What? Whatever did you find?'

'A wife! And Mother and I have come to ask whether she has changed her mind this morning.'

She began to smile.

'No, Monsieur, I never change my mind.'

It was then his turn to hold out his open hand, into which she dropped hers with a quick, decisive gesture. And he asked:

'As soon as possible, why not?'

'Whenever you like!'

'Six weeks?'

'I don't mind at all. What does my future mother-in-law think?'

Mme Roland answered with a sad little smile:

'Oh, I don't think anything. I'm only too thankful to you for having wanted Jean, for you will make him very happy.'

'I'll do what I can, Mother!'

Somewhat touched for the first time, Mme Rosémilly stood up, and taking Mme Roland in her arms kissed her for a long time like a child, and during this new kind of caress a powerful emotion made the poor woman's sick heart swell. She could not have described what she was going through. It was sad and sweet at the same time. She had lost a son, a grown-up son, and in his place had been given a daughter, a grown-up daughter.

When they were back in their chairs sitting face to face, they clasped hands and stayed like that, smiling at each other, while Jean appeared to be almost forgotten.

Then they discussed lots of things that had to be thought out before the impending marriage, and when everything was decided and settled Mme Rosémilly suddenly seemed to remember a detail, and asked:

'You have consulted M. Roland, haven't you?'

The same flush at once spread over the cheeks of both mother and son. It was the mother who replied:

'Oh no, there's no point!'

Then she hesitated, feeling that some explanation was called for, and went on:

'We do everything without telling him. It's enough just to say what we've decided.'

Mme Rosémilly was not in the least surprised, and smiled, thinking it quite natural because the old chap hardly counted.

When Mme Roland found herself back in the street with her son:

'Suppose we go to your flat,' she suggested. 'I could do with a rest.'

She felt homeless, with nowhere to go, being terrified of her own home.

They went to Jean's.

As soon as she knew the door was shut behind her she gave vent to a deep sigh as though the lock had guaranteed her safety, but then instead of resting as she had said she would, she began opening cupboards, checking piles of linen and numbers of handkerchiefs and socks. She altered the way things had been disposed of and tried to think out arrangements that looked more harmonious to her housekeeper's eye. When she had arranged things to her liking, put towels, pants and shirts on their special shelves, sorted all the linen into three main classes, personal, household and table, she stood back to contemplate her work and said:

'Jean, come and see how nice it looks!'

He got up and admired to give her pleasure.

When he had sat down again she tiptoed towards his chair from behind, and putting her right arm round his neck she kissed him and placed on the mantelpiece a small object wrapped in white paper which she had been holding in her other hand.

'What's that?' he asked.

She made no answer, but he understood as he recognized the shape of the frame.

'Give it to me!' he said.

But she pretended not to hear and went back to her cupboards. He stood up, quickly picked up this melancholy relic, crossed the room and double-locked it in the drawer of his desk. She wiped a tear from her eyes with her fingers and then said in a slightly quavery voice:

'Now I'll go and see whether your new maid keeps her kitchen tidy. As she is out now I can inspect it all and see for myself.'

Chapter 9

THE letters of recommendation from Professors Mas-Roussel, Rémusot, Flache and Borriquel, written in the most glowing terms for their student Dr Pierre Roland, had been submitted to the Board of the Transatlantic Company by M. Marchand and supported by Messieurs Poulin, judge in the Commercial Court, Lenient, the big shipowner, and Marival, Deputy Mayor of Le Havre and a particular friend of Captain Beausire.

It happened that no doctor had yet been appointed to the *Lorraine*, and Pierre was fortunate enough to be nominated in a few days.

The letter of appointment was handed to him by Joséphine the maid one morning as he was finishing dressing.

His first reaction was that of a man condemned to death who has been told that his sentence has been commuted: he felt his suffering had been immediately relieved a little by the thought of a departure and a calm life, always gently rocked by the rolling waves, always wandering, always going on.

He was now living like a silent and reserved stranger in his father's house. Ever since the night when he had blurted out to his brother the shameful secret he had discovered, he felt he had broken the last ties with his family. He was tortured by remorse for having told Jean this thing. He felt he was odious, unclean and wicked, and yet it was a relief to have spoken.

Never again did he look his mother or his brother in the eye. In order to avoid each other their eyes had developed an amazing mobility with the cunning of enemies afraid of crossing each other's path. He was always asking himself: 'What can she have told Jean? Has she admitted or denied it? What does my brother believe? What does he think of her and what does he think of me?' He could not guess the answers and it exasperated him. Moreover he hardly ever spoke to them now, except in the presence of Roland, so as to avoid these questions.

When he had received his letter of appointment he showed it the same day to the family. His father, who had a strong tendency to rejoice at everything, clapped his hands. Jean reacted in a serious tone but was inwardly full of joy:

'I do congratulate you with all my heart, for I know there was a lot of competition. You can certainly put it down to your Professors' letters.'

His mother looked at the floor and murmured:

'I'm very glad you have succeeded.'

After lunch he went to the Company's offices to find out about all sorts of things, and he asked the name of the doctor on the *Picardie*, which was due to sail on the following day, so as to ask him about all the details of the new life and the special things he would come up against.

Dr Pirette being on board, he went to see him and was welcomed into a small cabin by a young man with a fair beard who looked like his brother. They had a long talk.

In the reverberating depths of the great vessel there could be heard a great and continuous babel of sound, in which the thudding of cargo piling up in the holds mingled with the noises of footsteps, voices, machines loading crates, whistlings of boatswains and the jingling of chains being dragged along or wound on to winches by the raucous gasps of the steam engine which was making the whole fabric of the big ship vibrate.

But when Pierre had left his colleague and found himself back in the street, a fresh wave of melancholy came down on him like those fogs that roll over the sea from the distant ends of the earth, bearing in their intangible density something mysterious and impure, like the pestilential breath of far-off, evil lands.

Even in his times of deepest depression he had never felt so sunk in a foul pit of misery. It was because the final cord had been snapped and he had no connection left with anything.

Even while tearing from his heart the roots of all his affections he had not so far been through this lost-dog distress that had suddenly taken possession of him.

It was no longer a torturing moral pain, but the panic of an animal with no shelter, the quite physical anguish of a homeless, wandering creature, left to be assailed by rain, wind and storm, all the brutal forces of the world. By setting foot on this liner, by entering this tiny room tossed by the waves, his flesh, that of a man who has always slept in an immovable and quiet bed, had rebelled against the insecurity of all the days to come. So far this body of his had felt protected by the solid wall with foundations in the earth which supported it, and by the certainty of resting in the same place, under a roof that braved the tempest. But now everything that a man enjoys defying in the warmth of a sheltered home would become a peril and constant cause of suffering.

No ground under his feet any more but the rolling sea, roaring and engulfing. No space round him any more to walk in, run about and get lost in the byways, but a few metres of planking on which to tramp like a convict surrounded by other prisoners. No more trees, gardens, streets and houses, nothing but water and clouds. And he would feel the ship moving for ever beneath his feet. On stormy days he would have to hold on to partitions, cling to doors, claw on to the edges of his narrow bunk for fear of rolling off on to the floor. On calm days he would hear the whirring and vibration of the screw and feel the motion of this ship always carrying him on in a continuous, steady, maddening flight.

And he was condemned to this life of a wandering convict solely because his mother had given herself up to the embraces of a man.

He walked straight ahead, giving way to the desolate melancholy of men about to leave their homeland.

Gone from his heart was that lofty scorn and disdainful hatred of unknown passers-by. Now he felt a sad desire to speak to them, tell them he was about to leave France. and be listened to and comforted. In the depths of his being it was the shamefaced need of a poor beggar about to hold out his hand, a timid but deep need to feel that somebody else was sorry he was going away.

He thought of Marowsko. The elderly Pole was the only one who loved him enough to feel a real and keen emotion, and he at once decided to go and see him.

When he entered the shop, the chemist, busy pounding some powders in a marble mortar, gave a little start and left his task.

'Why don't we ever see you nowadays?' he asked.

The young man explained that he had had a lot of things to do, without disclosing to what end, and he sat down and asked:

'Well, how's business?'

Business wasn't going at all well. Competition was terrible, patients scarce and poor in this working-class district. You could only sell cheap remedies and doctors never prescribed the rare and complicated ones on which you can make five hundred per cent. The old boy concluded:

'If it goes on like this for three months more I shall have to shut up shop. If I weren't relying on you, my dear doctor, I should already have turned shoeblack!'

Pierre felt a pang in his heart and suddenly decided to deal the blow at once, as it had to be done:

'Oh, me . . . I can't be of any use to you in the future. I'm leaving Le Havre at the beginning of next month.'

Marowsko took off his glasses, he was so deeply moved.

'You . . . you . . . what do you mean by that?'

'I mean that I am going, my poor friend.'

The old man was thunderstruck, seeing his last hope crumbling, and he suddenly turned against the man he had followed here and whom he loved, in whom he had had so much confidence, and who was letting him down like this.

He stammered:

'But you're not going to betray me as well?'

Pierre felt so upset that he wanted to embrace him.

'But I'm not betraying you. I haven't found anywhere to

settle here and I'm off to be a ship's doctor on an Atlantic liner.'

'Oh Monsieur Pierre! You had promised so faithfully to help me to live!'

'What can I do? I must live myself. I haven't a penny of my own.'

Marowsko went on repeating:

'It's not right, what you are doing is not right. There's nothing left for me but to die of starvation. At my age it's the end. It's not right. You're abandoning a poor old man who came here because you did. It's not right.'

Pierre tried to explain, protest, give his reasons, prove that he couldn't have done anything else; the Pole would not listen, disgusted by this desertion, and he finally said, alluding possibly to certain political events:

'You French never keep your promises.'

Pierre jumped up, offended in his turn, and taking a rather lofty tone:

'You are unfair, M. Marowsko. You have to have very strong reasons for deciding to do what I have done and you should understand that. Good-bye. I hope I shall find you more reasonable next time.'

He went out.

'Ah well,' he thought, 'nobody will feel a sincere regret for me.'

His mind began running over everyone he knew or had known, and among these faces passing through his memory it lighted on that of the barmaid at the café who had made him suspect his mother.

He hesitated because he still bore her an instinctive grudge, but suddenly deciding that he would go he thought: 'After all, she was right.' And he looked about him to find the street.

It happened that the bar was full of people and smoke. Customers of all classes, for it was a public holiday, were calling out, laughing and shouting, and the boss himself was serving, rushing from table to table, taking away empty glasses and bringing them back capped with froth.

When Pierre had found himself a seat not far from the counter he waited in the hope that the barmaid would see and recognize him.

But she passed to and fro in front of him without so much as a glance, tap-tapping with tiny steps under her skirt and a nice little swing of the hips.

In the end he rapped on the table with a coin and she hurried over.

'What can I get you, Monsieur?'

She didn't look at him, for her mind was deeply involved with the cost of the drinks she was serving.

'Well, well,' he said, 'is that the way you talk to your friends?'

She looked at him and said in rather a hurry:

'Oh it's you. Are you all right? But I've no time today. It's a half for you?'

'Yes, half.'

When she brought it he went on:

'I've come to say my farewells. I'm going away.'

She answered with complete indifference:

'Oh really? Where?'

'To America.'

'They say it's a nice place.'

And that was all. Really he had been very ill-advised to talk to her that day. The café was much too crowded.

He went off towards the sea. As he reached the jetty he saw the *Perle* coming in with his father and Captain Beausire on board. Papagris the sailor was rowing, and the two men sitting in the stern were smoking their pipes with an expression of perfect bliss. As he watched them going past, the doctor thought: 'Blessed are simple souls.'

He sat down on one of the seats on the breakwater and tried to lull himself into an animal torpor.

When he got home in the evening his mother said, without daring to look up at him:

'You'll need all sorts of things to take away with you, and

I'm in a bit of a quandary. I've just ordered your underclothes and I have seen the tailor about other clothes, but do you need anything else, things I don't know about, perhaps?'

He was on the point of saying: 'No, nothing.' But he thought he ought at least to accept the means of getting some decent clothes, so he answered very calmly:

'I don't really know yet. I'll get details from the Company.'

He did so, and was given a list of indispensable things. When he handed it to his mother she looked at him for the first time for many a long day, and in her eyes there was the expression, so humble, gentle and imploring, of a poor beaten cur begging for pity.

On the 1st of October the *Lorraine*, coming from Saint-Nazaire, entered the port of Le Havre to set off again on the 7th for New York, and Pierre Roland had to take possession of the little floating cabin in which his existence would henceforth be confined.

The next day, as he was going out, he met his mother on the stairs where she was waiting for him, and she murmured in a scarcely audible voice:

'You wouldn't like me to help to make you comfortable on the boat?'

'No, thank you, it's all done.'

She whispered:

'I should so like to see your little room.'

'There's no point. It's very ugly and very small.'

He went on down the stairs, leaving her crushed, leaning against the wall, her face ashen.

But Roland, who went over the *Lorraine* that very day, talked of nothing else all through dinner but this magnificent ship, and expressed astonishment that his wife should have no wish to see her, since their son was going to sail in her.

During the following days Pierre hardly lived in the family at all. He was nervous, touchy, hard, and his cruel tongue seemed to lash everybody. But the day before his departure he suddenly seemed quite changed and very much softened. As he was kissing his parents before going off to sleep on board for the first time, he asked them:

'You will come and say good-bye on the boat tomorrow?'

'Good gracious yes, of course! Won't we, Louise?'

'Oh certainly,' she said, almost inaudibly.

Pierre went on:

'We sail at eleven sharp. You must be there at nine-thirty at the latest.'

'Oh,' said his father, 'I've an idea! When we leave you we can hurry and embark on the *Perle* so as to wait outside the jetties and see you once more. Can't we, Louise?'

'Yes, certainly.'

Roland went on:

'In that way you won't mix us up with the crowd that hangs about the mole when the transatlantics sail. You can't ever pick your own family out of the mob. Is that all right?'

'Oh yes, that's all right. That's settled.'

One hour later he was lying in his little sailor's bunk, as long and narrow as a coffin. There he lay for a long time with his eyes open, turning over in his mind everything that had happened in his life, and especially in his soul, during the past two months. Through having suffered and made others suffer his aggressive and vengeful distress had blunted itself like a worn-out blade. He hardly had the courage left to bear anybody any ill-will about anything, and he let his rebellion drift away like his whole existence. He felt so weary of struggling, weary of hitting out at people, of hating, indeed of everything, that he was incapable of anything further and tried to lull his heart into oblivion as one falls into sleep. He could vaguely hear the unfamiliar sounds of the ship around him, slight, hardly noticeable sounds in this calm night in harbour, and his wound, so cruel until then, left him with only the irritating little pains of its scarring over.

He had been sleeping soundly when he was awakened by the movements of sailors. It was daylight and the boat-train bringing passengers from Paris was arriving at the quayside.

Then he wandered about the ship among these busy, pre-occupied people looking for their cabins, calling each other, asking questions and answering them somehow or other in the general fuss of departure. After he had greeted the captain and shaken hands with his colleague the purser, he went into the saloon where a few English people were already dozing in corners. The huge room, with its white marble panels framed in gilt beading, multiplied indefinitely in its mirrors the perspective of long tables flanked by two endless lines of revolving chairs in crimson velvet. It was in fact the vast, floating, cosmopolitan hall in which the wealthy from all the continents were to dine together. Its opulent luxury was that of grand hotels, theatres and public places, the imposing, banal luxury that pleases the eyes of millionaires. The doctor was about to go on into the part of the vessel reserved for second class when he remembered that the previous night they had taken on a large herd of emigrants, and he went down into the steerage. As he went in he was assailed by a nauseous smell of poor and unclean humanity, a stench of bare flesh more sickening than that of the pelt or wool of animals. Then in a sort of dark, low tunnel like the gallery in a mine, Pierre saw hundreds of men, women and children stretched out on shelves one above the other or piled higgledy-piggledy on the floor. He could not make out their faces, but dimly saw this sordid, ragged crowd, this crowd of poor wretches defeated by life, exhausted, crushed, setting out with emaciated wives and ailing children for an unknown land where they hoped, perhaps, they wouldn't die of hunger.

As he thought of the past toil, the lost toil, the useless efforts, the pitiless struggle started afresh each day in vain, of the energy expended by this ragged lot who were about to begin again somewhere or other this existence of grinding poverty, the doctor felt like shouting out to them: 'Why the hell don't you chuck yourselves into the water along with your females and your young?' His heart was so wrung with pity that he couldn't bear to look at them and went away.

His father and mother, brother and Mme Rosémilly were already waiting in his cabin.

'You're early!' he said.

'Yes,' answered Mme Roland in an unsteady voice, 'we wanted time to see something of you.'

He looked at her. She was in black as though she had put it on for mourning, and he suddenly realized that her hair, which a month before was still grey, was now going quite white.

He had a job to seat the four people in his tiny home, and he himself jumped on to his bed. The door was still open, and through it they could see lots of people going by like a holiday crowd, for all the passengers' friends and an army of mere sightseers had invaded the huge liner. People were walking up and down the passages, in the saloons, everywhere, and heads were even poked into his cabin while voices murmured: 'That's the doctor's quarters.'

Pierre then pushed the door to, but as soon as he felt shut in with his family he wanted to open it again, for the bustle of the ship covered up their awkward silence.

Mme Rosémilly at last made an effort to say something:

'You don't get much air through those little windows,' she said.

'That's a porthole,' Pierre explained.

He showed her the thickness of the glass that made it capable of resisting the most violent batterings, then went at great length into the locking system. It was now Roland's turn to ask a question:

'Have you got your dispensary in here?'

The doctor opened a cupboard and showed them a collection of bottles with Latin names on squares of white paper.

He took one out and enumerated the properties of its contents, then a second and then a third, and gave a real lecture on pharmacology which they appeared to be following with rapt attention.

Roland frequently remarked with a shake of the head:

'Now isn't that interesting!'

There was a gentle tap on the door.

'Come in!' called Pierre.

Captain Beausire appeared.

He shook hands all round and said:

'I have come late because I didn't want to intrude when you were overcome by emotion.'

He had to sit on the bed too. A fresh silence fell.

But suddenly the Captain cocked an ear. Through the partition he could hear orders being given, and he announced:

'It's time for us to be off if we want to embark on the *Perle* so as to see you again as you leave and bid you farewell on the open sea.'

Roland senior was very much set on this, no doubt to impress the passengers on the *Lorraine*, and he jumped up with alacrity.

'Well, good-bye, my boy.'

He kissed Pierre's whiskers, then opened the door.

Mme Roland did not move but sat there with downcast eyes, looking very pale.

Her husband touched her arm.

'Come along, hurry up, we haven't a minute to spare.'

She stood up, took one step towards her son and proffered one waxen cheek and then the other, which he kissed without a word. Then he shook hands with Mme Rosémilly and his brother, and asked him:

'When is your wedding to be?'

'I don't know yet for certain. We'll make it fit in with one of your trips.'

At length they all left the cabin and went up to the deck which was cluttered with visitors, porters and sailors.

The steam was snorting in the great belly of the ship which seemed to be shaking with impatience.

'Good-bye,' said Roland, still in a hurry.

'Good-bye,' answered Pierre, standing by one of the little wooden gangways connecting the *Lorraine* with the quay.

He once again shook hands all round and his family moved off.

'Quick, quick! let's get into the cab,' shouted Father.

A cab was waiting for them and took them to the outer harbour where Papagris had the *Perle* in readiness to put to sea.

It was one of those dry, calm autumn days, without a breath of air, when the smooth sea looks as cold and hard as steel.

Jean seized one oar, the sailor put the other into position and they began rowing. On the breakwater and jetties and even on the granite parapets a huge, milling, noisy crowd was waiting for the *Lorraine*.

The *Perle* passed between these two waves of humanity and was soon beyond the mole.

Captain Beausire, seated between the two women, held the tiller and was saying;

'You'll see, we shall be just on her course, just there!'

The two rowers pulled with all their strength to get as far as possible. Suddenly Roland called:

'There she is. I can see her rigging and two funnels. She's coming out of the inner harbour.'

'Come on, hearties!' cried Beausire.

Mme Roland took her handkerchief out of her pocket and dabbed her eyes.

Standing and clinging to the mast, Roland announced:

'At this moment she is turning in the outer harbour . . . She is standing still . . . She's moving again . . . She must have taken the tow-rope from her tug . . . She's moving, hooray! . . . Now she's between the two jetties . . . Can you hear the crowd yelling bravo! . . . It's the *Neptune* towing her . . . I can see her bows now . . . There she is, there she is . . . Lord, what a boat! . . . Oh Lord, just look at her!'

Mme Rosémilly and Beausire turned round, the two men stopped rowing, Mme Roland was the only one not to move.

The huge liner, hauled by a powerful tug that looked like a caterpillar in front of her, was emerging from the harbour slowly and majestically. The people of Le Havre, massed on the moles, on the beach and in the windows, carried away by a burst of patriotism, began to shout: 'Long live the *Lorraine*!' acclaiming and applauding this magnificent departure, like a great maritime city giving birth to her most beautiful daughter and presenting her to the sea.

But She, as soon as she had passed through the narrow passage between the two granite walls, feeling herself free at last, dropped her tug and set off all alone like an enormous monster galloping over the waters.

'Here she is! Here she is!' Roland was still yelling. 'She's coming straight at us!'

Beausire, radiant, kept on saying:

'What did I promise you, eh? Don't I know their course?'

Jean said softly to his mother:

'Look, Mother, she's coming.'

Mme Roland uncovered her tear-stained eyes.

The *Lorraine* was coming full steam ahead now she was clear of the harbour, and the weather was fine and calm. Beausire clapped his glass to his eye and announced:

'Look! M. Pierre is in the stern, quite alone and easy to see. Look!'

Lofty as a mountain and fast as a train, the ship was now going past, almost touching the *Perle*.

Mme Roland, distraught and beside herself, held out her arms towards it, and she saw her son, her son Pierre, wearing his braided cap, throwing farewell kisses to her with both hands.

But he was going, rushing away, disappearing, already quite tiny, gone like an imperceptible dot on the gigantic vessel. She struggled to pick him out still, but no longer could.

Jean had taken her hand.

'You saw?' he said.

'Yes, I saw. How good he is!'

They turned back towards the town.

'Golly! She travels fast!' declared Roland with enthusiastic conviction.

And indeed the liner was shrinking from second to second as though melting into the ocean. Mme Roland sat turned towards it and watched it going over the horizon towards an unknown country at the other end of the world. On that boat, which nothing could stop, that boat which she would lose sight of in a moment, was her son, her poor son. It seemed to her as though half her heart was going with him, that her life was over; it also seemed as though she would never see her child again.

'What are you crying about?' asked her husband. 'After all, he'll be back again in less than a month.'

She stammered out:

'I don't know. I'm crying because I don't feel well.'

When they had landed, Beausire left them at once to go and have lunch with a friend. Then Jean walked ahead with Mme Rosémilly, and Roland said to his wife:

'He really is a fine looking fellow, is our Jean!'

'Yes.'

And as she was too upset to think of what she was saying she added:

'I am so happy that he is marrying Mme Rosémilly.'

The old boy was thunderstruck.

'Eh, what's that? He's going to marry Mme Rosémilly?'

'Yes, of course. We were going to ask your opinion this very day.'

'Well, well! How long has this been on the cards?'

'Oh, not long. Only for a few days. Jean wanted to be sure she would accept him before consulting you.'

Roland rubbed his hands.

'Very good, very good. That's capital! I most heartily approve.'

As they were about to leave the quay and go along the boulevard François I, his wife turned back once again to take one last look at the open sea, but she could see nothing but a wisp of grey smoke, so distant, so faint that it looked like a light mist.